Sacrifice of Darkness

Also From Alexandra Ivy

GUARDIANS OF ETERNITY
When Darkness Ends
Embrace the Darkness
Darkness Everlasting
Darkness Revealed
Darkness Unleashed
Beyond the Darkness
Devoured by Darkness
Bound by Darkness
Fear the Darkness
Darkness Avenged
Hunt the Darkness
When Darkness Comes
Darkness Returns
Beware the Darkness
Conquer the Darkness
Sacrafice Of Darkness

BAYOU HEAT SERIES
Raphael/Parish
Bayon/Jean-Baptiste
Talon/Xavier
Sebastian/Aristide
Lian/Roch
Hakan/Severin
Angel/Hiss
Rage/Killian (1001 Dark Nights)
Michel/Striker
Ice/Reaux
Kayden/Simon (1001 Dark Nights)
Blade (1001 Dark Nights)

THE IMMORTAL ROGUES
My Lord Vampire
My Lord Eternity
My Lord Immortality

Sacrifice of Darkness

A Guardians of Eternity Novella

By Alexandra Ivy

1001 DARK NIGHTS

PRESS

Sacrifice of Darkness
A Guardians of Eternity Novella
By Alexandra Ivy

1001 Dark Nights

Copyright 2020 Alexandra Ivy
ISBN: 978-1-951812-15-7

Foreword: Copyright 2014 M. J. Rose

Cover photo credit © Annie Ray/ Passion Pages

Published by 1001 Dark Nights Press, an imprint of Evil Eye Concepts,
Incorporated

Acknowledgments from the Author

To the men in my life who keep me sane. David, Chance and Alex.
I love you!!

One Thousand and One Dark Nights

Once upon a time, in the future…

*I was a student fascinated with stories and learning.
I studied philosophy, poetry, history, the occult, and
the art and science of love and magic. I had a vast
library at my father's home and collected thousands
of volumes of fantastic tales.*

*I learned all about ancient races and bygone
times. About myths and legends and dreams of all
people through the millennium. And the more I read
the stronger my imagination grew until I discovered
that I was able to travel into the stories… to actually
become part of them.*

*I wish I could say that I listened to my teacher
and respected my gift, as I ought to have. If I had, I
would not be telling you this tale now.
But I was foolhardy and confused, showing off
with bravery.*

*One afternoon, curious about the myth of the
Arabian Nights, I traveled back to ancient Persia to
see for myself if it was true that every day Shahryar
(Persian: شهریار, "king") married a new virgin, and then
sent yesterday's wife to be beheaded. It was written
and I had read that by the time he met Scheherazade,
the vizier's daughter, he'd killed one thousand
women.*

*Something went wrong with my efforts. I arrived
in the midst of the story and somehow exchanged
places with Scheherazade — a phenomena that had
never occurred before and that still to this day, I
cannot explain.*

*Now I am trapped in that ancient past. I have
taken on Scheherazade's life and the only way I can
protect myself and stay alive is to do what she did to
protect herself and stay alive.*

*Every night the King calls for me and listens as I spin tales.
And when the evening ends and dawn breaks, I stop at a
point that leaves him breathless and yearning for more.
And so the King spares my life for one more day, so that
he might hear the rest of my dark tale.*

*As soon as I finish a story... I begin a new
one... like the one that you, dear reader, have before
you now.*

Prologue

Human architects and artists had created a beautiful tribute beneath the city of Athens. The underground stoas were a hidden labyrinth of shops and villas—and even some temples. The beauty, however, paled in comparison to the grandeur demons created in the subterranean tunnels buried deep in the ground.

The sprawling fight club was built of rare marble with arched doorways that led to vast rooms filled with a wide variety of entertainment. Water sprites splashed among the sparkling fountains, and naked imps sprawled on velvet pillows for any vampire in need of blood.

Or anything else they might hunger for.

Even the actual fighting pit had been built in the style of an elegant amphitheater—a cage in the center, and marble seats sweeping upward in the shape of a fan. It was all very civilized. Except for the air that pulsed with thick, savage violence.

Leaving the pit–still covered in the blood of his latest opponent– Javad the Vanquisher strolled through the corridors with their fluted columns and heavy tapestries that depicted his rise as a fighter. He couldn't remember each and every battle that had been embroidered on the heavy velvet. Still, he had a vivid memory of the first time his sire, Vynom, had placed him in a fighting pit. The orc he'd been about to battle had laughed at the sight of Javad in a simple loincloth, his dark hair pulled back, and his hands empty. The creature had assumed that Javad needed weapons to be dangerous. Javad had swiftly taught him the error of his ways.

The battle had ended when Javad ripped the tusk out of the male's mouth and used it to slice open the orc's chest, destroying the heart.

Stories of the gruesome victory had spread far and wide. Within a few decades, Vynom had abandoned the small demon club to create a larger, more exclusive establishment, offering the opportunity for demons to wager vast sums of money on their ability to defeat Javad the Vanquisher. They'd become successful beyond their wildest imaginings.

Lately, however, it didn't feel like success to Javad. In fact, everything had started to feel like a prison. And in some ways, it was.

From the moment Javad had awakened as a vampire, Vynom had stressed the importance of loyalty. He reminded Javad over and over that most sires abandoned their offspring before they ever rose from the grave. And that Javad would be dead or roaming the mountains of Persia alone and feral if Vynom hadn't taken him into his lair. It had been he who'd taught Javad to survive as a vampire. He who'd protected him when they were attacked by a roving band of hellhounds. He'd also honed Javad's fighting skills.

And any time Vynom feared that he hadn't fully earned his undying obedience, he used fists, whips, and even silver chains to bend Javad to his will.

Now, he was so indoctrinated, believing that he owed Vynom his very soul, that the mere thought of walking away caused him physical pain.

Grinding his fangs that still ached from the beating he'd taken from the vicious troll mongrel, Javad ignored the clutch of demons that surrounded him. Most of them were the usual admirers who attended each battle and desperately hoped to gain his notice. However, a few vampires were also there, trying to convince Javad to leave Vynom to fight for them.

They were like flies buzzing around him, refusing to leave even after he waved them away.

Turning into the hallway that led to his private rooms at the back of the club, Javad frowned when he caught sight of a large demon pressing something—or someone—against the wall.

Rastiv.

The nasty goblin had a square head that sat atop a bullish body. His features were brutish, and he had the manners of a... Well, the truth was, he didn't have any couth. He was a depraved animal that should have been locked in the nearest dungeon. Unfortunately, Vynom enjoyed keeping a few savages around to maintain order. The fights stirred the mob of demons to a fever-pitch, not to mention the amount of money won and lost during each battle. They needed some sort of crowd control.

But a few weeks before, Javad had discovered Rastiv attempting to force himself on a water sprite. He'd warned the goblin that the next time he caught him behaving like a monster, he would throw him out of the club. Obviously, the idiot hadn't taken his threat seriously.

Now, Javad shoved aside the slender imp currently trying to attract his attention and moved to grab Rastiv's shoulder. At the same time, he glanced toward the female, who pressed herself tightly against the wall, watching him with large eyes.

An emotion he'd never experienced before detonated inside him.

Javad hissed, feeling oddly dizzy. What the hell was happening? He'd taken a thousand blows during his years as a fighter. Never once had he felt as if his knees were going weak. Nor had his head spun.

Shocked by the intensity of his reaction to the unknown female, he allowed his gaze to sweep over her delicate features framed by thick, honey-colored curls. Her eyes were the most amazing shade of lavender, her nose a narrow blade. Her lips a lush invitation.

He tilted back his head, absorbing her scent. Aloe vera? He frowned. Who was she?

And why the hell did he feel an overwhelming urge to toss her over his shoulder and carry her to his private rooms?

Annoyed by the unexpected emotions that churned within him, Javad dug his fingers into Rastiv's shoulder and jerked him around.

"I warned you what would happen the next time I caught you forcing yourself on a female."

Rastiv scowled, his thick skin covered with scales, and tusks sticking out of his lower jaw.

"Nymph, mine," he grunted. The tusks were formidable weapons, but they made it difficult for the male to speak.

Nymph? Javad's gaze shot toward the female. She looked like a nymph, but there was something…else. Some power he could sense but couldn't name.

"Tough. I told you to let her go."

"No." The goblin grabbed the hilt of the war hammer he had strapped around his broad waist. Almost as if he was stupid enough to try and challenge Javad. "Mine."

Javad narrowed his gaze. "I gave you an order."

"You go 'way." Rastiv grabbed his dick in a lewd gesture. "I make female scream."

The nymph made a small sound of terror, and Javad's anger combusted into a blinding fury. He told himself it was because he hated creatures that abused those smaller and weaker than themselves. Perhaps ironic, considering that he was a fighter. But he never entered the cage with an unwilling opponent.

It wasn't until he felt the earth shake beneath his feet that he suspected this was more than just anger at the goblin being a disgusting pig. Damn. He usually maintained iron-clad control over his ability to cause small earthquakes. No one wanted tons of rock collapsing on their head. Losing control meant that his emotions must be nearing their breaking point.

Javad sought the lavender gaze, holding it for just long enough to ensure that it was imprinted on his memory. Then, slowly, he turned to face Rastiv.

"I warned Vynom that you were an undisciplined liability," Javad drawled. "You've proven me right."

The goblin scowled. Big words tended to confuse him. Of course, putting his shoes on the correct feet tended to confuse him.

"Me fighter." He pounded his chest. "Me *best* fighter."

Ah. Javad allowed a cold, humorless smile to curve his lips. Any creature who had to boast they were the best, proved that they weren't. And Rastiv was obviously chafing at the knowledge he would always be second-best.

Javad reached out, grabbing Rastiv's tunic. Then, with the strength that had made him the most feared warrior in the world, he picked the goblin off his feet and tossed him across the narrow space.

A smattering of laughter sounded from the nearby crowd as Rastiv smashed into the wall with enough force to crack the marble, but Javad barely heard their twittering. He was entirely focused on the infuriated goblin as he jumped to his feet and lowered his head.

He didn't know why Rastiv wasn't scurrying away. Perhaps the creature had convinced himself that he was capable of defeating Javad. Or, more likely, he hoped to impress the onlookers. The idiot had always been jealous of Javad's fame.

It didn't matter to Javad. He spread his feet, anticipation coursing through his body. He was going to make Rastiv pay for every second he'd terrorized the beautiful nymph.

Every. Single. Second.

Chapter 1

Javad was renowned throughout the demon world. Over the past century, he'd created a posh, outrageously elite demon club. The Viper's Nest in the heart of Vegas was by invitation only, and creatures literally begged on their knees for an opportunity to walk through the doors. Some he let in. Most he didn't.

Most of his customers would be shocked to discover that he hadn't started his existence in elegant surroundings.

They had no idea he'd been hauled from one seedy pigsty to another. Barren caverns, crypts, lava pits, and sweltering swamps. His sire, Vynom, had taken Javad around the world, using Javad's skills as a fighter to accumulate a fortune.

He was intimately familiar with the congested noise, the filth, and the explosions of violence that were mandatory for most demon establishments. What he'd forgotten was the pungent stench.

Walking through the door of the Diablo Club, the smell hit him like a physical punch. Unwashed bodies. Rotting food. Blood. The club was only across town from the Viper's Nest, yet it seemed a world away.

Wrinkling his nose, Javad glanced around the dark, narrow room that was crammed with customers. There were several fey creatures, along with trolls and goblins and even a few vampires. Like a variety pack of demons.

The urge to turn on his heel and walk away vibrated through Javad. He'd put these sorts of places behind him. Thank the goddess. Of course, the reason he was here was because of his past.

So…irony at its finest.

Tilting his head back, Javad ignored the stench and tested the air.

He wasn't stupid enough to waltz through this crowd without making sure there weren't any unwelcome surprises.

The ground shook beneath his feet as he released a sudden burst of power. He easily recognized a familiar scent.

"Uze," he muttered, his fangs now fully extended.

He'd threatened to kill the slave trader if he ever returned to Vegas.

With effort, Javad regained command of his temper. He silently promised himself he'd deal with the mongrel troll later. One lowlife at a time. Javad returned his attention to the other demons, confident there was nothing nearby that could kill him. At least not without a fight.

Heading toward the back of the room, Javad strolled through the crowd that parted to give him plenty of space. Even with his fangs hidden and no weapon in sight, the customers managed to sense that he was the most dangerous creature in the club.

A few bold females reached out as he passed. Javad was used to their eager attempts to capture his attention. It wasn't arrogance to admit that he was fascinating to other demons, because it wasn't personal. Just one of the benefits of being a vampire.

And it didn't hurt that he was tall and slender with sculpted muscles that rippled beneath his black slacks and crimson silk tunic that fell to his knees. His dark hair was glossy in the muted torchlight and long enough to brush his shoulders. His face was lean, and his features were uncompromisingly stark as if they'd been chiseled from stone. And unlike many vampires, his skin held a rich color. He'd spent too many years in the brutal desert sun before being turned to entirely lose the glorious sheen.

At the moment, his eyes were dark with sensual invitation, the primitive method of luring his prey. But when he was angry, they shimmered a bright bronze. He was told that they smoldered with enough power to send grown trolls fleeing in terror. On the side of his neck was a stylized tattoo that revealed he'd been an assassin during his life as a human.

At last, Javad reached a small male nearly hidden in the thick shadows at the back of the club. The creature had a bald head and weirdly gaunt features. As always, he wore a loose robe that covered his body from neck to toe. His eyes were dark as a harpy's wing, but at the very center, a crimson flame burned like the pits of Hell.

"Rupert," Javad said as the demon tried to sink deeper into the inky blackness.

Rupert was a mongrel rompo, something Javad suspected he managed to conceal from most creatures who visited his club. Rompos were the scavengers of the demon world, turning into skeletons to feed on corpses. Most species considered them to be the lowest of lifeforms and detested them.

Javad didn't mind them. Hey, someone had to be the bottom-feeder of the gene pool.

"Don't start with me, leech. Not all of us have your prejudices against slave-traders, and Uze spends his money freely," Rupert warned, his voice coming out as a strange purr. "I don't tell you how to run your club. You can keep your damned nose out of mine."

Javad waved his hand in an impatient gesture. "I'm not here about the slaver."

"Then what do you want?" Rupert looked suspicious.

Javad didn't hesitate. "Information."

"About what?"

"Fighting pits," Javad told him. "Somewhere in the desert."

"A fighting pit?" The demon ran his fingers over his bald head, widening his eyes with faux innocence. "Seriously?"

"Do I look like I'm kidding?"

"Never heard of any."

Javad stepped forward. An air of suppressed violence vibrated around him. It wasn't just his position as manager of the Viper's Nest that made him the top demon in Vegas. It was the power that thundered through him. Even now, the building trembled beneath shockwaves of energy. Only Chiron, one of the rebel vampires who ran a casino that catered to humans, could hope to match him in strength. It was one of the reasons they tended to avoid each other.

"Think hard, Rupert." Javad's voice was barely above a whisper. "Think very, very hard."

"I don't have to think," Rupert purred, stupidly ignoring the threat hanging in the air. "I don't know anything about any fighting pits around here."

Javad's hand moved with the speed of a striking snake, his fingers wrapping around the demon's throat.

"Wrong answer." Javad peeled back his lips to expose his fangs.

"Argh."

"Still the wrong answer." Javad's fingers tightened until the male's face turned a weird shade of dark red.

A roar sounded behind them, and Javad glanced toward a troll who was lumbering in their direction.

"Tell your goon to stay back," Javad warned, tightening his fingers until the demon's face turned an even darker shade of puce.

Hmm. Pucier?

The rombo desperately gestured toward the large demon, who stumbled to a puzzled halt. Javad turned back to Rupert.

"Now, one last time. Tell me where I can find the fight club."

"It's out in the desert someplace," the male choked out, gasping for air.

"Be more specific."

Dark eyes flared with crimson flames. "I can't. It's always moving. Plus, it's hidden behind layers of illusion."

"Who runs it?"

"I don't know."

Javad lifted the demon until his feet dangled off the floor. Behind them, the troll growled in fury, but he wasn't stupid enough to try and interfere.

"You never learn, do you?" Javad smiled. "Give me a name before I start ripping off body parts. Starting with that lump of flesh between your legs."

That did it. Males were males, no matter what their species. Start threatening the family jewels, and they would betray their own mother.

"A vampire called Vynom." Rupert coughed, his breath wheezing through his crushed throat. "And before you ask, I've never talked to the male, he's never visited this club, and I've never been to the pits."

Javad allowed the creature to dangle off the floor for another minute, then he dropped him with a flick of his wrist. For the moment, he would accept that Rupert was telling the truth. If he discovered he was lying, he could always kill him later.

"Who has been to the pits?"

Rupert regained his balance, glancing toward the crowd of rowdy demons. Javad suspected that he was more interested in hiding the crimson flames in his eyes than checking out his customers. Those eyes would reveal his heritage and stir up awkward questions.

"None of these losers," the bar owner muttered. "Only the most elite fighters are invited."

Javad abruptly turned and headed toward the door. The name Vynom had hit him with stunning force. He didn't want anyone to detect his unwelcomed sense of vulnerability. All demons were predators. They would strike the second they suspected any sort of weakness.

Besides, he'd just caught a familiar scent. One that he hadn't expected in this seedy establishment.

Keeping his pace slow and steady, Javad retraced his steps out of the club, pretending to ignore the numerous demons who watched him leave with speculative gazes. Then, following the surprising scent, he rounded the side of the low building to glare at the vampire leaning against the crumbling stucco.

Viper. Clan chief of Chicago. And Javad's current master.

The male had long, silver hair as pale as the moonlight and dark eyes that held a mocking amusement. His face was lean and far too perfect to be anything but a vampire. And while he wasn't as tall as Javad, he was equally slender. Tonight, he was dressed like a Regency dandy, in a dark green velvet coat and silk pants, with a lacy white shirt. He should have looked ridiculous. Instead, he was as regal as any king.

Javad folded his arms over his chest. "What are you doing here?"

Viper arched a brow. "Hello, Javad. Wonderful to see you. How are you? Good, I hope. And me? Why I am in excellent health." He ran a slender hand down the emerald pile of his coat. "Is that a new jacket? Why yes, it is. A gift from Shay. Thanks for noticing."

Javad rolled his eyes. Viper's sense of humor was almost as peculiar as his choice in fashion. Of course, when you were eternal, you had the luxury of dressing however the hell you wanted. Trends and fads had no meaning. "Since when do you care about manners?"

Viper pretended to be shocked. "You wound me, old friend. I am infamous for my exquisite charm."

"Only when it earns you money."

"Shay has been trying to civilize me."

Shay was Viper's mate. Javad had met her on several occasions and genuinely liked the Shallot demon. But while she might have many fine qualities, he doubted *anyone's* ability to civilize Viper.

"Have you told her that it's a wasted effort?"

Viper smiled, his long fangs shimmering in the light of the flashing neon sign above the building.

"She lives in eternal hope."

"Why are you here?" Javad repeated his question. As much as he enjoyed the company of his master, he was anxious to start his hunt.

Viper shrugged. "I wanted to check on the club."

Javad believed that Viper had traveled to Vegas to visit the Viper's Nest. The male liked to keep his finger on the pulse of all his businesses, even those that were wildly successful. But that didn't explain why he was standing outside the Diablo.

"Your GPS must be malfunctioning. The Viper's Nest is across town."

"My GPS is just fine. Candace told me you were here. And why."

Damn. Javad was going to have strong words with his second in command. The female vampire was usually loyal to the point of fanaticism. Although, to be fair, Viper was her ultimate master.

"I don't need a babysitter."

"Do I look like a babysitter?"

Javad grimaced. His master might possess a glossy sophistication that fooled the humans, but just below the surface was a ruthless demon that had survived endless challenges to his position as clan chief. Only a fool would assume he was anything but a lethal predator.

A soon-to-be dead fool.

"Viper—"

"How about a friend?" Viper interrupted. "Could you use a friend?"

Javad hesitated. His brutal past made it difficult to lower his barriers. Viper was one of the few who'd managed to earn his trust. And that had taken several centuries.

He gave a slow nod. "Yeah. I could use a friend."

"I could only hear a portion of your conversation with the rompo demon. There's a fighting pit in town?"

A familiar fury blasted through Javad. When he'd finally walked away from the pits, he'd sworn that he would do everything in his power to make sure no other demon suffered as he had.

"In the desert."

"And you're going to close it down?" Viper demanded.

"I made the law that fighting pits are forbidden in my territory. If I don't take action, it will make me look weak."

Viper eyed him with a grim expression. "And it has nothing to do with the fact that Vynom is the one running it?"

Javad's fangs lengthened. Just the thought of his sire was enough to stir his most savage impulses. With effort, he forced himself to shrug with fake indifference. If Viper realized the depths of Javad's hatred for the male who'd abused his loyalty for centuries, he would do everything in his power to halt Javad's fierce thirst for revenge.

"His presence is a direct challenge to my authority," Javad said in icy tones.

Viper wasn't satisfied. "You're the boss in Vegas. Send one of your employees to deal with the bastard. You pay them to take out the trash, don't you?"

"Vynom's not particularly powerful, but he's cunning and utterly immoral. I'm not going to risk my staff."

Viper arched a brow. "And that's the only reason you insist on being the one to go after him?"

Javad met Viper's smoldering dark gaze. There was no way to lie. The older vampire knew him too well.

"No, that's not the only reason."

"Javad, you're one of the most frightening warriors I've ever known," Viper said in somber tones. "And that's saying something."

It was. This male was best buds with Styx, the King of Vampires. The towering six-foot-five Anasso was rumored to have enough power to collapse entire cities. Something Javad had done once or twice in the past.

"But?" Javad prompted.

Viper reached out to touch the small medallion that was hung around Javad's neck. The older male understood that it was Javad's most prized possession even if he didn't know the reason.

"But emotions are the enemy of any fighter. This is too personal." Viper murmured. "If you don't want to send one of your people, then I'll deal with Vynom."

Javad knew his master was right. The grinding hatred he felt toward his sire was bound to cloud his judgement. But there was no way in hell he was going to allow anyone else to confront the male who'd tortured and abused him to make a fortune.

"This meeting is overdue. I have to deal with my former master once and for all." Thankfully, Javad's voice was calm. "For my own sanity."

There was a long silence as if Viper were considering the likelihood of talking Javad into letting him deal with Vynom. At last, accepting that he would have better luck stopping the sun from rising, Viper lowered his hand and stepped back.

"First, you have to find the club," he reminded Javad. "It'll be protected by illusions."

Vampires had many powers, but sensing magic wasn't one of them. "I have several fey on the payroll. They should be able to locate the place."

"I have something better," Viper assured him.

"What?"

"Not what. Who."

Javad frowned. Was Viper referring to his mate? He hadn't heard the beautiful demon had a special talent for finding illusions…

Abruptly, Javad realized exactly who Viper meant.

"No." He shook his head in violent repudiation. "Oh, no."

Viper grimaced. "I hate to admit it, but he's the best. If you're serious about confronting your old master, you need to find those pits before Vynom discovers you're coming to destroy him."

Shit. Javad's shoulders slumped. Viper was right. If he wanted to catch his sire by surprise, he had to locate him before anyone discovered that he'd been asking questions.

"Fine," he growled. "Have him meet me at the Viper's Nest. But, if he's not there by midnight, I'm leaving without him."

A slow, mysterious smile curved Viper's lips.

Three hours later, Javad understood his master's wicked sense of amusement. The older vampire hadn't been able to convince Javad to give up his thirst for revenge. Still, he *had* managed to ensure that the journey was as uncomfortable as possible. No, wait. *Uncomfortable* didn't cover his time spent in the company of the miniature gargoyle.

Aggravating on an epic scale was more apt.

Levet claimed to be a gargoyle, but he was less than three feet tall with gray, leathery skin, stunted horns, and large, fairy-like wings that shimmered in brilliant blues with crimson and gold. Javad suspected the creature had been sent from the netherworld specifically to torment any demon unfortunate enough to cross his path.

Mile after mile, the gargoyle had led him across the hard-packed earth, his mouth never shutting. He claimed to be a knight in shining armor who saved the world regularly. He spoke of his close and personal connections to the King of Vampires as well as the new Queen of the Merfolk, who he described in tedious detail.

Then there were the endless questions.

Did Javad personally choose who could enter the club? Did Javad cheat at cards? Did Javad know Elvis…

"Are you deliberately leading us in circles?" Javad snapped at last as they rounded a Joshua tree that he was certain they'd passed an hour before. Did they all look exactly the same?

Levet glanced over his shoulder, his brow furrowed. "Why would I lead us in circles?" he asked with a slight French accent.

Javad scowled. "Because you're an aggravating pest."

The creature stuck out his tongue before returning his attention to the low line of hills just ahead of them.

"We are close," he said.

Javad glanced around with a strange prickle of unease. He'd been in Vegas long enough to spend time in the desert. But his visits were usually spent tracking down a customer who owed him money or feeding on one of the sand sprites who lurked among the scrub brush near the edge of the city. He hadn't wandered through the vast emptiness, completely exposed.

It was unnerving.

"That's what you said twenty minutes ago," he reminded the gargoyle.

The fairy wings fluttered with what Javad assumed was irritation. "I cannot concentrate if you are forever napping at me."

Napping? Javad frowned before giving a resigned shake of his head. "Nagging?"

"*Oui*. Yak, yak, yak."

The ground shook as Javad struggled to contain his temper. It should have been easy. He'd devoted centuries to gaining complete mastery over his emotions. It was the one thing he *could* control. But something about the stunted creature set his fangs on edge.

"You—"

"This way," Levet rudely interrupted, waddling toward a large rock formation that rose from the desert floor like a skyscraper.

"I'm going to have a long conversation with Viper when I get back to Vegas," he growled, reluctantly following the creature. It wasn't like he had much choice. He couldn't find the pits without Levet.

"When you talk to him, would you remind the leech that it was not my fault that his silly car ran off the road and into a pole? I could not know a cat would wander into the street as I was turning the corner." He clicked his tongue. "He has been a poopy-head for weeks."

Javad muttered a startled curse. Levet had taken one of Viper's beloved cars on a joyride? Christ. Grown orcs wouldn't be that brave.

"You have more courage than brains," he muttered. "Of course, that's not saying much."

Levet ignored him as he halted next to the rock formation. "There is an illusion here."

Javad moved to stand next to the gargoyle. He couldn't see anything but rocks. He would need a beacon specifically tuned to vampires to lead him through the illusion. Or a three-foot gargoyle, who was giving him a headache.

"Is it the pits?"

Levet wrinkled his nose. "It smells like pits. Why are they always so stinky?"

Javad could tell the gargoyle that the smell came from a toxic brew of fear and hate and desperation. Instead, he squared his shoulders, anticipation surging through him.

At last. Reaching up, he touched the medallion hung around his neck.

Vynom was about to die. Justice would be served, not only for himself, but also for all the innocents who'd suffered because of the male's insatiable greed.

"Let's go."

"Wait." Levet abruptly reached out to grab Javad's arm.

Javad shook off the tiny hand, growling in frustration. "What's wrong?"

Levet sniffed the air. Then, without warning, he scrambled backwards. "It is a trap."

The words had barely left the gargoyle's mouth when the ground opened up and swallowed them whole.

Chapter 2

Terra strolled through the gardens, hoping their beauty would ease the restless ache in the center of her soul. It was annoying. She'd spent centuries struggling to squash these abrasive sensations that left her nerves raw.

When she was young, she'd resented everything about the Seraf temple. It didn't matter that being born with such rare healing abilities was considered the greatest honor among the nymphs. She hated the isolation. The fact that her destiny had been chosen for her. And most of all, she loathed the knowledge that her burgeoning abilities were being wasted.

It'd taken a near disaster for her to accept that the protection of the temple was necessary. Over the years, she'd managed to find beauty in the lush gardens that surrounded her home. And, of course, there was joy in healing the handful of petitioners the Matron approved.

But the restless dissatisfaction had never gone away.

In fact, it'd grown progressively worse.

Annoyed with her futile frustration, Terra turned away from the small lake that glittered beneath the constant sunlight and threaded her way through the tangle of wildflowers that filled the air with a sweet perfume.

As she passed, the small, vivid blooms seemed to reach out to her. She couldn't exactly talk to them, but they whispered a song in her ear.

Trying to focus on the peace that drenched the isolated pocket between dimensions, Terra reached the back of the temple. The delicate structure surprised the rare visitors who were allowed to visit. Since the veils that protected the temple were dauntingly thick, most of them expected to find some sort of grim fortress.

Instead, the temple was shaped like a giant tower chiseled out of smooth crystal. The peak was tall enough to disappear into the distant clouds, and the base was wide enough to contain a small village. There were also dozens of chambers beneath the ground for visitors who were allergic to sunshine.

Terra paused, using her magic to create an opening in the crystal before entering the public lobby. The vast, open space was empty beyond the delicate chairs that were woven from branches, and the rugs that covered the tiled floor. It wasn't unusual. Terra could go days without encountering anyone. The temple was large enough to house thousands of Serafs. Currently, there were less than fifty of them in residence.

Serafs had once lived in the world. They traveled from village to village, offering their gifts to whoever needed healing. Then rumors that the blood of a Seraf could protect demons from any harm, no matter how grievous, had started to circulate, and they'd been hunted like animals.

In a desperate attempt to salvage the handful of Serafs that were left, they'd gathered together and used their magic to create the temple. But even then, they continued accepting anyone who arrived on their doorstep. During a plague, they might have thousands of sick demons crowded into the temple.

As time passed, however, they'd become more and more reclusive. The temple had been locked away from the world, and the petitioners had trickled to a small, select handful.

A handful that Terra was beginning to suspect had paid an enormous fee to be healed.

Intending to spend a few hours in the library, Terra was startled by the sudden appearance of a slender female with delicate features and eyes the color of spring grass. Her hair was dark gold and braided to hang down her back. Like Terra, she wore a flowing white gown, and her feet were bare.

At a glance, the two looked similar. They both possessed the delicate beauty of all nymphs. However, Terra's hair was closer to honey than gold and left free to tumble down her back. And her eyes were an astonishing lavender color. They also shared the soft scent of aloe vera.

Terra offered a nod of her head. "Cyra," she murmured in soft tones.

Cyra was one of the few older Serafs still willing to speak to Terra. The others had branded her a rebel. They didn't like the questions she asked or her insistence that the temple of the Serafs was there to serve others, not to accumulate wealth or power. Or maybe it was her influence among the younger healers who shared her desire to reach out to those in need that angered the elders. In any case, they tended to regard her with cold disdain.

"I have been searching for you," the female said.

Terra blinked in surprise. "Really? Is there a petitioner?"

"Not exactly," Cyra said.

"I don't understand."

Cyra reached into the pocket of her robe and pulled out a medallion that hung from a delicate golden chain.

"I was given this by…" Her words trailed away as if she were reluctant to say the name. "By a sister. She claims that it appeared on the doorstep this morning."

Terra frowned in confusion. Nothing could get through the barriers around the temple.

"How did it get here?"

Cyra arched a brow. "You tell me."

"Me?" Terra looked closer, her breath suddenly tangling in her throat as she realized that she recognized the medallion that was lying in the middle of Cyra's palm. She should. It had once belonged to her. "Javad," she whispered.

"A friend of yours?"

A strange sensation darted down Terra's spine as the thought of the vampire seared through her mind. With vivid detail, she could conjure the image of his lean, beautiful features, his satiny dark hair, and the fathomless black eyes that shimmered with a bronze glow when his emotions were heightened. It'd been centuries since she'd last thought of the male, but now, the memories flooded through her as if they'd broken through a barricade.

And in a way, they had. She'd built up protective layers to block out the time she'd spent in Vynom's clutches. Including any memories of Javad.

Cyra held out her hand. "How did he come to possess your medallion?"

Instinctively, Terra reached to take the necklace. "It was a long time ago. I'd almost forgotten."

Staring down at the medallion that was carved with an image of the tower, Terra became briefly lost in the emotions swirling through her.

"Terra?"

With a blink, she lifted her head to discover the older woman staring at her with a hint of concern.

She swallowed a sigh. She'd done her best to burrow her head in the sand and pretend that it'd all been a bad dream. Now, it was time to confront her past.

"Maybe we should sit down," Terra suggested.

"Very well." Cyra led them to a low sofa that had been arranged to overlook the gardens.

They settled on the woven seats together, and Terra hesitated. She had the words. She was just struggling to push them past her lips.

At last, Cyra reached to grasp her hand, giving Terra's fingers a small squeeze.

"Take your time."

She drew in a deep breath and slowly released it. Then, stiffening her spine, she forced herself to speak.

"You probably remember when I was first brought to the temple. I wasn't very happy."

Cyra was polite enough not to laugh at the gross understatement. Terra had still been young and emotional and filled with arrogance. She'd been stronger than all the other healers and convinced her skill gave her some unique wisdom. She'd been wrong.

"Ah." Understanding flared through Cyra's eyes. "I remember now. Didn't you disappear for a time?"

A shudder raced through Terra. "Yes. I thought I could teach the Matron that we belonged among the people. A stupid mistake that nearly cost me everything." She reached up, touching her shoulder. Beneath the silk of her robe was an ugly brand that marred her skin.

"What happened?"

Terra concentrated on the feel of Cyra's warm touch. The Serafs could not only heal the body but also the mind.

"Less than a day after I ran from the temple, I was captured by a band of trolls," she admitted.

Cyra gasped. "Oh no."

It'd been terrifying. Terra's smug belief that she could easily survive on her own had been shattered as she sought shelter in a small glade. One minute she'd been heading toward the narrow stream of water. The next, she was being crammed into an iron box with three other nymphs.

Terra glanced toward the gardens, her mouth dry. "I feared they were going to kill me and drink my blood."

Cyra gave Terra's fingers another squeeze before releasing her hand. "What did they do?"

"They held me prisoner for months. Eventually, they sold me to a vampire named Vynom." Her jaw tightened, an ancient fury flowing through her blood. "He ran a fighting pit in Athens."

Cyra looked confused. "You were put in the fights?"

"No, I wouldn't have lasted more than a few seconds." A feeling of sickness rolled through her belly. She'd spent her life sequestered among a tribe that was devoted to peace. The sight of the demons savagely trying to tear each other to bloody shreds had been a shocking introduction to the real world. "They were vicious."

"What did the vampire want from you?"

"My skills as a healer."

Cyra tilted her head to the side. "I don't understand. Our healing powers don't work on vampires."

"I was used to heal the other demon fighters," Terra explained. "Or at least I healed the ones who could afford the obscene fees demanded by Vynom. It allowed them to keep fighting even after their opponent had gained the upper hand."

"That doesn't seem fair."

Terra released a humorless laugh. The abuse of her healing powers had been the least horrid thing that had happened during those dreadful nights.

"There was nothing fair about that place. It catered to the most violent monsters to walk this Earth." Sickness continued to churn in her belly. "Most matches were to the death. And at the end…" The words stuck in her throat as images of mutilated demons gasping in the center of the pit assaulted her.

"Terra?"

Terra cleared her throat. She wanted to be done with her explanation so she could shove the memories back where they belonged. In the past.

"At the end of the night, the winner of the most bouts had the opportunity to face Javad," she said.

Cyra nodded toward the necklace that was clutched in Terra's hand. "The Javad who held your medallion?"

"Yes."

"He was a warrior?"

Terra slowly shook her head. The moment she caught sight of Javad entering the fighting cage, she'd known he was different. It wasn't just because his dark beauty had stolen her breath. No, her gift of healing allowed her to sense his soul. There was none of the savage lust that lay like a shroud of malice over the other demons.

Her instinct had been proven right when, just a night later, he'd brutally beaten a goblin who'd been pressing her against the wall with the intent of raping her. The violent display had kept away any other demon who might think she was easy prey.

"Against his will," she told her companion. "Javad was a victim. Like me."

Pity darkened Cyra's eyes. "He was forced to fight?"

Terra nodded. "His sire, Vynom, was a nasty, cruel vampire who treated Javad like a dog." Terra clenched her hands into tight fists. Just the thought of Vynom was enough to send a toxic brew of emotions bubbling through her. "No, he treated him worse than a dog. The vampire didn't care whether Javad lived or died as long as the monsters would pay to watch him fight. And worse, he used Javad's own need to please his sire to hold him captive."

"Oh, Terra," Cyra breathed. "You must have been terrified."

Terra swallowed a lump in her throat. She could almost smell the blood and fury and death that soaked into the dark pits beneath the streets of Athens.

"At first, I wanted to curl into a ball and die," she admitted with brutal honesty. "It was only the stolen moments I could spend with Javad that allowed me to maintain my sanity. Eventually, not even that was enough. I became angry. So angry with the violence and blood. And needless death." With effort, she forced her hands to unclench. "That's when Javad appeared like a guardian angel to help me escape. I think he sensed I'd reached a point where I would do anything to be free. Even if it meant ending my life."

"He saved you," Cyra murmured.

No one had been more shocked than Terra when Javad had unlocked the door to the cell where Vynom kept her imprisoned. He hadn't said a word. Instead, he'd motioned for her to follow him. She hadn't hesitated. Not even for a second. She'd instinctively trusted the male as he led her through a hidden door and into the human sewers. He'd been her only friend since she'd left the safety of the Seraf temple. With a small push, he'd urged her to flee into the darkness, ignoring her urgent pleas for him to come with her.

It wasn't until she was far away that she realized that he must have done something to the guard who was always posted in front of her cell. And no doubt several more that were patrolling the hallway. Vynom hadn't survived in his ugly, savage world by accident. He took his security very seriously.

"Yes, and he risked his life to do it," she said.

Cyra studied her. "So you gave him the medallion."

Terra nodded. After Javad had refused to escape with her, she'd taken the medallion from around her neck and pressed it into his hand.

"I promised if he ever had need of me, he was to hold the medallion and speak my name." A rueful smile twisted her lips. "Then I scurried to the temple as fast as I could run."

There was a long pause as Cyra considered her words. Then she stretched out her hand to touch the medallion that Terra was absently stroking between her fingers.

"This is a pledge," she said.

"Yes."

"Serafs are supposed to break all connections to the outside world. It's our oath."

Serafs were expected to offer their gifts without concern for whether the demon in need was friend or foe. Which meant any loyalties they had before coming to the tower had to be purged.

"I had nothing else to offer. And honestly..." Terra grimaced as her words faded.

"You didn't think he would use it," Cyra suggested in gentle tones.

Terra shuddered, regret twisting her heart. "I know it's awful, but it seemed impossible to believe that Javad could survive more than a few years at the most."

"What will you do?"

"What should I do?"

Cyra's expression was impossible to read. "If the Matron discovers you've left the temple, she will punish you. Perhaps even have you put in the dungeons."

Terra grimaced. The Matron had been seeking any means to discredit Terra and put an end to her uncomfortable questions. If Terra left the temple, it would give the older female the perfect opportunity to banish her.

Then again, nothing said the Matron had to discover that she'd left...

"This is your choice, my child," Cyra said, rising to her feet. Then, as if able to read Terra's mind, she offered a secretive smile. "I will tell you that the Matron is expecting an important visitor in a few days. She invited several sisters to join her for a formal dinner, which means she'll be preoccupied with overseeing the preparations."

With that, the older female walked away. Terra watched her leave, battling through her tangled emotions.

She'd made a solemn oath to the Serafs to devote her life to healing.

She couldn't break that sort of oath and not expect repercussions.

On the other hand, how could she turn her back on Javad? Without his assistance, she had no doubt she would be dead. Or worse. She owed him everything.

Rock. Hard place.

Spinning on her heel, Terra headed back into the gardens. Entering one of the private grottos, she clutched the medallion she'd given to Javad in her hand. Then, making sure that no one could see her from the temple, she closed her eyes and allowed the memory of the lean, perfect male face to form in her mind.

"Take me to him," she whispered.

Chapter 3

Javad landed at the bottom of the cavern, using the top of his head to break his fall. The blow not only knocked him out but when he finally clawed his way back to consciousness, his brain felt like scrambled eggs.

He felt sudden sympathy for Humpty Dumpty.

Shaking his head, Javad tried to rid himself of the sluggish sensation. A mistake. The movement sent sharp pains through his injured brain. Damn. It'd been a long time since he'd cracked his skull. Not since his days in the fighting pits.

With a grimace, Javad forced open his eyes and glanced around.

He wasn't surprised to discover that he was in a small, barren cell that looked as if it'd been chiseled out of the hard granite. Above him, the magical opening had closed to become a thick, impenetrable ceiling. And at the far end, a heavy silver door was set into the stone.

Had he stepped into a trap deliberately set for him? Or was it a general security system designed to keep demons from entering the fights without an invitation? And where was the aggravating gargoyle?

His foggy thoughts were abruptly forgotten when he caught the scent of rusted iron.

Vynom.

Javad caught the familiar sound of his sire's heavy tread as the male vampire halted outside the cell. Javad's former master stood six-foot-five, as tall as Styx the King of Vampires, with the same type of bulky muscles. He could make the ground shake when he walked. But his innate powers didn't match his physical strength. Actually, he was one of the weakest demons Javad had ever known. To compensate, Vynom had become a cunning bully who used manipulation, deceit, and an utter lack of anything resembling morals to build his empire.

Javad surged upright. He would have to be dead not to meet his former master on his feet. At the same time, he reached for the silver dagger he'd holstered beneath his tunic before leaving Vegas.

Gone. Shit.

Vynom opened the door and entered the cell. His bald head gleamed in the muted light from the corridor, and his pale, square face looked as if it had been carved from the same gray granite as the cell. He wore a loose linen shirt that had a deep vee to reveal his broad chest and worn leather pants. Javad arched his brows. The last time he'd seen his ex-master, the male had been wearing the finest silks and velvets and drenched in gold and gems.

"Ah, my son. I've been waiting for you to drop in." Bright green eyes glittered with mocking amusement and something else. Something Javad couldn't decipher. "What took you so long?"

Javad folded his arms over his chest, pretending he hadn't noticed that he was standing in the middle of a cramped cell.

"I was debating whether to come myself or send one of my servants." He shrugged. "As Viper pointed out, it's my underlings' responsibility to deal with the trash."

"Viper." The name was spat like a curse. Clearly, no love lost between the two ancient vampires. "How is your new master?"

"Successful. Sane. Deliriously happy with his new mate."

Vynom's lips twisted with unmistakable envy. "I suppose good things happen when you're the Anasso's favorite pet. Personally, I've never been willing to kiss ass to get what I want."

"No, you just brutally torture those you should be protecting," Javad taunted.

"Brutally torture? That's a little melodramatic, isn't it?"

"Says the male who never stepped into the fighting cage."

Vynom shrugged. "I'm a capitalist who understands that we all have our skill sets. Mine is to make lots of money. Yours is to make creatures bleed."

Javad clenched his fangs. Vynom had a unique ability to piss him off. He couldn't afford to be goaded into losing his temper right now, though. Not when he didn't know how he'd gotten into the cell. Or how the hell he was going to get out.

Instead, he lazily glanced around his barren surroundings. Fighting pits were always dirty and smelly and chaotic. Still, as Vynom's fortunes had risen, he'd started taking pride in hosting his battles in elegant establishments. He chose the grandest cities and recreated the architectural style of the local palaces. It was a subtle way to make the demons attending the fights feel as if they were royalty.

"Looks like your skill set is slipping," Javad goaded his sire. "Since when do you host competitions in dusty holes in the middle of the desert?" He returned his gaze to the older vampire, taking in the male's simple clothing. "And since when do you dress like a cast member from *Les Misérables?*"

The vampire's green eyes flared with fury, the scent of rust becoming choking in the air. Then, clenching his hands into tight fists, Vynom struggled to regain command of his temper.

"I'll admit, there have been setbacks since you abandoned me. But that's all about to change."

"Is it?"

"Yes," Vynom assured him. "You, my son, are about to replenish my empty coffers."

Dread curled in the pit of Javad's stomach. "Doubtful."

"It's already been arranged."

"What has?"

"The fight of the millennium."

"Fight of the millennium?" Javad rolled his eyes. It sounded like a cheesy reality show. Or an 80s band. "Catchy."

"And true."

"Yeah, well, good luck with that."

"I don't need luck." Vynom stepped forward, a smile curving his lips. "Just you in the cage."

"Just me? Damn. I'm more popular than I realized. Do you want me to sing a song or do a dance?" Javad mocked. "I'll warn you that I'm tone-deaf, but my singing is still better than my dancing."

"I want you to battle against Frack. To the death."

Frack. Acid curled through Javad's stomach. The massive orc had been fighting for centuries. Not only was he a full-blooded orc who stood over seven feet tall, he also had plates of armor magically embedded in his skin to protect his vital organs. And he was nucking futs. When he wasn't in the cage to fight, his owner kept him shackled and chained to the wall to prevent him from creating utter carnage.

The ground shook beneath his feet. It was Javad's power, however, that caused the small quakes. Unlike Vynom, who weighed as much as a small tank.

"Not gonna happen."

Vynom took a step back. He was greedy, immoral, and brutally selfish, but he wasn't stupid.

"It's already scheduled," he informed Javad. "In fact, the crowd started arriving last night. They're eager to watch the epic return of Javad the Vanquisher."

Javad pulled back his lips to reveal his fangs. "Don't call me that."

"And even more eager to bet shitloads of treasure on the outcome."

Javad narrowed his eyes. "They can bet all they want. I'm not fighting."

Vynom looked smug, but Javad didn't miss the male's quick glance over his shoulder. Was he expecting someone? Frack? Elvis?

"I think you will," Vynom muttered.

"Do the threats of torture come now?" Javad asked. "Hot pokers? Silver chains? Listening to you reminisce about the good old days?"

"Actually…" The male's words trailed off as the sudden scent of fresh aloe vera swirled through the cell. Then, without warning, a female seemed to appear out of thin air and dropped to the floor. "Ah. Just in time," Vynom drawled.

Javad ignored his former master, his gaze locked on the female he hadn't seen in centuries.

"Terra."

With a fluid motion, Javad crouched down and reached out to lightly touch her throat. Relief jolted through him at the steady beat of her pulse.

Once assured that she was alive, he allowed his gaze to sweep over her delicate face. Oddly, it was as familiar as if they'd parted ways yesterday. Perhaps because he'd allowed himself to recall every sweep and curve of her elegant features on a regular basis. *Too* regularly.

He knew the precise shade of honey in the long curls that tumbled over her shoulders. The shocking beauty of her lavender eyes that were currently hidden behind a thick fringe of dark lashes. The plush pink of her lips. The only obvious change was the flowing white gown that pooled around her like melting snow.

Javad shook off his strange sense of…what? Destiny? No, that couldn't be right.

It has to be anger, he sternly told himself. He'd spent centuries reminding himself of all the reasons he would never see this female again. Now, she'd somehow been sucked into this hellhole. It was only natural for him to be furious.

Of course, that didn't explain the tingles of excitement that buzzed and sizzled through his body.

Jerking up his head, he glared at his former master. "What have you done to her?"

"Nothing." Vynom held up his hand. "It's a side effect of coming through the magical barrier, nothing more. You see?" He pointed toward Terra as her lashes fluttered open. "I'll leave the two of you to get reacquainted for an hour or so. Then you'll need to prepare to fight. I'm sure after all this time, you'll want the opportunity to practice and work out the kinks. I can't have you giving my customers a subpar performance."

Javad jutted his chin. "I'm not fighting."

Vynom smiled with cruel anticipation. "You fight. Or the female dies. Your choice."

* * * *

Levet had watched helplessly as Javad dropped like a stone to the bottom of the cavern. He, on the other hand, had managed to avoid being sucked down as if he were in a massive toilet. Hey, it was not his fault that vampires didn't have the good sense to possess wings.

Unfortunately, he was still entangled in the spell and unable to escape. Desperately releasing a burst of magic, he sent himself sailing through a narrow crack in the nearest wall.

For a breathless second, he thought he'd managed to avoid any unpleasant repercussions from the cleverly concealed trap. He zoomed through the darkness at an exhilarating speed, expecting to shoot out of the caves and into the desert. Instead, he smacked painfully against a stalactite and plunged to the ground.

Or was it a stalagmite?

Not that it mattered. Who cared what they called the pointy rocks that filled the dark, musty cave?

Feeling decidedly ruffled to have been tossed around like a piece of radish—no, wait…rubbish, Levet struggled to get to his feet. Then, grabbing his tail, he polished the tip to a smooth gloss. It soothed his nerves, and of course the females adored a shiny tail, did they not?

Once his delicate nerves were settled, he cast a quick glance around. He was obviously in a remote part of the cavern complex. The hard, dusty floor was devoid of footprints, and silence lay thick in the darkness. There wasn't even the rancid scent of fighters that usually contaminated the fighting pits.

He stilled. That was not entirely true. There was a smell. It wasn't rancid, but instead a dry, crisp scent. Levet tilted back his head and took a deep sniff. *Oui*. There it was. Very faint, but unmistakable.

"*Bonsoir*," he called out. "Who is there?" He waited. Nothing. "I can smell you."

There was a soft beat of wings, then a small female stepped from behind a pointy rock.

"Don't hurt me," she pleaded in a voice as soft as snowflakes.

Levet blinked, studying the tiny creature. She was shorter than him with a slender body barely hidden beneath a gown made of gossamer lace. Her hair was long and so pale it almost looked white, while her features were astonishingly delicate with big, gray eyes.

Not long ago, Levet would have been enchanted by the pretty creature. He was a male who appreciated females of all sorts. Tall or short. Young or old. Slender or curvaceous. Now, however, he had developed a taste for a large ogress with mermaid blood, gaudy muumuus, and a bad temper. It was rather annoying, but what could a poor gargoyle do?

"Why would I hurt you?" he asked in confusion.

"Everyone hurts me."

"Not *moi*."

The female inched forward, studying Levet with a suspicious gaze. "You promise?"

Levet placed his hand in the center of his chest. "Cross my knees and hope to die," he promised. "Well, I do not truly hope to die."

She continued forward, halting directly in front of him. "What are you?"

Levet scowled. "What a silly question. I am a gargoyle, of course. Do you not see my horns and my lovely wings?"

"Um…right. A gargoyle." She cleared her throat. "Forgive me. I meant to ask, *who* are you?"

Levet clicked his tongue. That was an even sillier question. How was it possible she did not recognize him? He was famous.

"I am Levet." He performed a dashing bow, spreading his wings so she could admire the brilliant colors. "Knight in shining armor and savior of the world. More than once."

She tilted her head to the side. "That is quite a title for such a small creature."

Levet straightened. "Size is all relative."

"True." She drifted closer. "I am Sparkle."

Levet nodded. It was a name that suited the tiny creature. "What are you?"

"A frost fairy."

"Frost?" Ah. That explained the shimmer that coated her pale skin, and her dry, crisp scent. But as far as Levet knew, they never left their lairs in the Arctic. Had she wandered into the caverns? "Are you lost?"

She shook her head. "I was kidnapped from my home. Now I am trapped here."

"Oh." That made more sense. "Who trapped you?"

"Vynom."

Levet wrinkled his snout. He had never met Javad's sire, but he already disliked the leech. Any creatures who ran fighting pits or slave markets were... What did his friend Shay call them? Bottom breeders? *Non.* Bottom feeders.

"Why did he trap you?" he asked.

Her sparkly wings drooped. "He uses me as bait."

"Bait for what?"

"To excite the crowds," she said, her voice trembling. "He has a maze he created at the other end of the caverns. Before the main battles begin, he places me in the maze and releases a pack of hellhounds. The crowd can wager on whether I'll reach the end before the hellhounds eat me."

It wasn't often that Levet was speechless.

He'd started his life with his dear mother trying to kill him, followed by being sold into the slave pens. And just a few years ago, he'd confronted the ultimate evil trying to destroy the world.

Hard to be shocked after that.

But the mere thought of this fragile creature being used to incite the bloodlust of a pack of savage demons made his tummy feel icky.

"That is horrid," he muttered.

Her wings drooped another inch. "Yes."

Levet glanced around the cave. He couldn't sense any guards. Or any spells that might keep the female trapped.

"Why do you not escape?"

"These caverns are surrounded by magic," she told him. "You can easily enter, but you can't leave. Not without the permission of Vynom."

Levet frowned. He hadn't considered the possibility that he might be stuck down here.

"That is not good. I have business elsewhere. I cannot wait around for some nasty leech to open a doorway."

Sparkle glanced around as if making sure they were alone, then she leaned toward Levet to speak in a soft voice.

"There might be a way."

"A way to what?"

"Escape."

Levet's spidey senses started to tingle. "If you had the means to escape, why are you not already gone?"

She did another of those look-arounds. Then she stepped closer to Levet. "There is a collapsed tunnel at the end of the maze. The magic is weakest there," she told him. "If we could dig through the rocks, I believe we could escape. I don't have the strength by myself."

Levet remained skeptical. A beautiful fairy suddenly appearing to offer him the opportunity to escape seemed like a plot twist from one of those cheesy late-night movies he adored. He'd learned the hard way that if something seemed too good to be true, it was always a trick. Usually, a nasty one.

"Hmm," he murmured.

"Do you want to get out of here?" she asked, a hint of impatience in her gray eyes.

Levet hesitated. Of course, he wanted out. He did not like dark, dusty holes in the ground. More importantly, he had a number of tasks on his to-do list.

A dinner date with Shay while she was visiting Vegas.

A standing poker game with a pack of curs who had more money than brains.

And an appointment for a seaweed facial scrub along with a

Brazilian wax.

He wanted to look his best when he returned to the merfolk castle.

But he wasn't in the mood to waltz into a trap. And a niggling voice in the back of his head kept telling him that he should go and look for Javad. Not that it was his duty to rescue the leech, but he was a knight in shining armor. It was his duty to help others.

Heaving a resigned sigh, he at last decided that he had no choice but to follow the frost fairy and discover if she was telling the truth. If she was right and there was a way to get out of the caverns, then he would search for Javad. They might need the male's brute strength to clear the passage.

"Lead the way."

Chapter 4

Terra blinked away the darkness that clogged her mind. What had happened? One minute she'd been stepping through a portal. And the next, she'd been knocked out.

Cautiously, she took in her surroundings. She was lying on a hard floor that felt like stone. Heavy darkness pressed against her and indicated that she was in some sort of underground space. But a cool power also brushed over her like a breeze.

Terra stiffened, and the familiar scent of saffron and raw male desire teased her nose. She turned her head to discover the vampire kneeling over her.

"Javad," she breathed, tingles of pleasure exploding through her.

She hadn't forgotten her physical reaction whenever she caught sight of the lean, perfect face. Of how those dark, smoldering eyes made her blood heat and her stomach twist with anticipation. But she'd told herself that it had more to do with the emotional trauma of being held hostage in the fighting pits. Everything was more intense when she was in a constant state of terror.

Now, she realized she'd only been fooling herself.

The sparks and flutters and breathless excitement were just as acute as ever. No, even more so, she realized as she forced herself into a sitting position.

She didn't know where she was, or if they were in danger, or even if Javad was injured. But every instinct she had screamed at her to wrap her arms around him and never let go.

Instead, she contented herself with devouring him with her gaze, taking in every delicious inch of him. From the top of his glossy, dark hair and down the hard body covered by his familiar silk tunic and pants. Her mouth went dry, and her heartbeat thundered by the time her gaze returned to his face, sweeping over the starkly chiseled features.

"Where are we?" she finally managed to croak.

"In a cavern beneath the Mojave Desert," he told her. "How did you get here?"

She frowned. Why would they be in the Mojave Desert? And why was Javad staring at her as if he were troubled by her arrival?

"I used a portal."

"Yes, but why?"

Her frown deepened. Had Javad taken a blow to the head?

"You called to me, don't you remember?"

He slowly shook his head. "What are you talking about?"

"With this."

Terra grabbed the chain around her neck, pulling it up to reveal the medallion hidden beneath her robe.

With a muttered curse, Javad jerked his hand up to touch his neck as if searching for something that wasn't there.

"How did you get that?"

Terra moved so she was kneeling, directly facing Javad. She couldn't heal a vampire, but she might be able to clear the obvious confusion from his mind.

"It arrived at the temple this morning."

He hissed in anger. "Someone must have taken it off me while I was laying here unconscious. The same time they stole my dagger."

"Impossible. Only you could have used the magic to return the medallion to me."

"Me?" He sent her a fierce glare. "I would never have done that."

Terra flinched, shockingly hurt by his response. Not only his insistence that he hadn't used the medallion but also the seeming horror at the mere thought of seeing her again.

"I…see." She bowed her head, hiding the stupid tears that filled her eyes. "Sorry. My mistake."

There was silence, then she felt the soft brush of Javad's fingers over her hair. "Terra, do you want to know how many times I've held that medallion in my hand and longed to speak your name?" His voice was low and harsh with unexpected emotion. "Just to see your face. Or hear your voice."

She shivered. "You don't have to make excuses."

His fingers moved to cup her chin. "Look at me, Terra. Please." He waited for her to reluctantly lift her head and meet his steady gaze. "Surely you remember my arrogance?"

She did. She used to watch Javad, amazed by the crowds of demons who scampered to get out of his path whenever he strolled through the club. His confidence had vibrated the air around him, containing enough power to make the earth shake. Terra had instinctively remained in the shadows, but astonishingly, he always sensed her presence, pausing to offer her a mysterious smile.

More than once their gazes had met and held. And held. For what seemed like an eternity, they would simply stare at each other, a strange sense of awareness settling in the center of Terra's soul. She'd accepted that wasn't just another frightening warrior who inhabited the pits. He was fascinating and exotic and so sexy, her knees had gone weak.

A wistful smile touched her mouth. "It's hard to forget."

His thumb absently brushed her lower lip, his eyes dark with memories. Were they the same as hers? The thought made her muscles clench with a hunger she'd tried so hard to forget.

"Then you know that I say exactly what I think," he murmured. "I've never stopped thinking about you. Just as I've never stopped rejoicing in the knowledge that you were safe in your temple, performing the healing you were born to do."

"I…"

Terra's words died on her lips. For centuries, she'd complained that the Serafs were failing in their duties. She was convinced that her sense of restlessness had been caused by the knowledge that they should be opening their doors to anyone in need of their skills, not just those who could offer some sort of reward.

Now, she felt a niggling fear that a portion of her agitation was a direct result of missing this male. Could her devout desire to spread their healing around the world have been inspired by her gnawing hunger to return to Javad?

So much for the purity of my cause, she wryly acknowledged.

With effort she thrust away her unwelcomed insight. Now wasn't the time to be distracted.

"So how could the medallion have gotten to the temple?"

Javad started to shake his head, only to stiffen as if he'd been struck by sudden inspiration.

"Vynom."

Terra wrinkled her nose in disgust. Even after all this time, she still had nightmares about the brutal vampire who'd held her captive.

"I thought I could smell him."

"These are his fighting pits." Javad's voice held an edge of ancient bitterness. "He said he'd been expecting me. Not surprising since he deliberately intruded on my territory. It was easy to assume that I would show up to shut down his business since I've outlawed fights."

An unexpected jolt of joy raced through Terra as she realized what he was saying. She'd spent all this time terrified that Javad was still in Vynom's clutches, enduring one punishing battle after another until he simply couldn't recover. Then she glanced around, really taking in her surroundings, and a portion of her joy dimmed. She'd initially assumed they were in Javad's private quarters. A closer inspection revealed the heavy silver door across the cramped space.

A cell.

"This is your territory?"

His lips twisted at her hesitant question. "Not the fighting pits. I manage a demon club in Vegas. We fulfill demon fantasies without violence."

Ah. Terra nodded. She could easily imagine Javad in command of an elegant establishment like that. He'd always possessed an instinctive sophistication that was out of place in the pits.

"Does it make you happy?"

"I've found…" He paused as if searching for the right word. "Peace. Something I never expected."

"I'm glad." Unable to resist temptation, she leaned forward and touched his face.

A mistake. Instant, ruthless need sizzled through her. As hot and molten as lava. Which was ironic really, considering his skin felt like cool silk beneath the tips of her fingers. Icy and smooth, and dangerously addictive. A growl was wrenched from her throat. She wanted to run her hands over his entire body. To explore every hard inch…

Javad's eyes shimmered a stunning bronze, his snowy white fangs lengthening as he reacted to the scent of her desire. Leaning forward, he brushed his lips down the length of her jaw before nuzzling the corner of her mouth.

"You are very distracting," he murmured.

Terra shuddered, her stomach cramping with intense pleasure. It'd been so long since a male had touched her. Not since Javad had kissed her goodbye in the sewers beneath Athens.

Now, her entire body was going up in flames.

"Am I?"

He scraped the tip of one fang over her lower lip. "Yes." His arms started to wrap around her, only to freeze when a distant scream of pain sliced through the silence. "Damn. The fall must have cracked my skull," he muttered in self-disgust, leaning back. "Now isn't the time to indulge in fantasies."

Terra wanted to do a little screaming herself. She *wanted* to indulge in fantasies. After spending endless nights dreaming of being in Javad's arms, his fangs sinking deep into her throat, she ached for his touch.

Unfortunately, he was right.

She didn't know why they were there, but it couldn't be good. Kidnappings didn't usually involve fun and games. More like pain and torture.

"So, Vynom brought you here?" she asked, once again glancing around the cell.

"Yes. Just as he brought you here."

She returned her attention to Javad's grim expression. "I told you, that's impossible. The medallion is directly bonded to you."

"Impossible or not, Vynom knew you were about to enter the cell."

Terra parted her lips to argue, then grimaced. As she'd matured, she no longer assumed that she knew everything. A rare benefit of aging.

"If that's true, he must have some means of perverting our magic," she said.

"He's good at perverting things," Javad reminded her in dry tones.

Terra tucked the medallion and chain back beneath her gown and rose to her feet. She didn't have the answers. And for now, she had more pressing matters that needed her attention.

"I'll have the Matron see if she can determine how he used the medallion."

Javad straightened, standing next to her. "Can you get us out of here?"

"Of course." She lifted her hand, intending to form a portal to take them to the temple. From there, she would find a means to return Javad to his home.

The magic tingled through her, but as soon as it hit the heavy air, it sputtered and died. Like a flame being smothered.

What the heck?

She tried again. And again. And again. Her heart sank at the familiar sense of impotence. She'd been caught in this snare before.

Javad lightly touched her shoulder. "Terra?"

She sent him a worried glance. "The portal forms, but it won't open on the other end. Just like the first time I was trapped by Vynom."

* * * *

"The bastard," Javad growled. "He must have a witch who created a mire spell."

"Is it the same spell he used in Athens?"

"No. That was a dampening spell that prevented any magic inside the lair. Vynom didn't allow his fighters to use spells or incantations. This is targeted to keep anyone from leaving. It's easy to get in. Impossible to get out." Javad clenched his hands at his sides. He'd been infuriated to be led into a trap as easily as a drunken ZuZu demon. But now that Terra was stuck in this cell—not to mention, in danger—his rage was incandescent. Only the knowledge that he'd collapse the entire cavern complex if he didn't keep his emotions in check allowed him to stay in control. "Like a quagmire."

"So we're stuck here?"

He grimaced. "Momentarily."

Terra slowly nodded. Her lavender eyes were dark with concern, but just like in the past, her expression remained calm. He'd always been amazed by her ability to maintain her serenity even when surrounded by chaotic violence.

"Why would he bring us here?"

"He needs money," Javad said without hesitation. In some ways, Vynom was a simple creature. Nothing mattered but cold hard treasure.

Terra furrowed her brow. "Does he think the temple will pay a ransom for my return?"

"No. He knows he can't force me to fight. Not without leverage."

"What leverage?" Terra's eyes widened with sudden horror. "Me?"

There was no use trying to deny it. "Yes."

Terra considered his explanation. "That doesn't make any sense," she finally announced. "We haven't seen each other for centuries. Why would he assume you even remember me?"

Javad swallowed the urge to laugh. Not remember her? Each and every second he's spent with her was seared into his brain. The way the torchlight had danced over her honey hair. The mysterious beauty of her lavender eyes. Her soft, aloe vera scent. The memories had haunted his dreams.

And he didn't doubt that Vynom had sensed Javad's fascination with the fragile young Seraf. Perhaps even realized that it was more than just the lust of a male for a beautiful female.

Not something Javad wanted to discuss with Terra when they were stuck in a filthy cell at the bottom of a cavern.

"I finally found the backbone to walk away from Vynom a few decades after you returned to the temple," he said, knowing exactly how to distract her. "He must realize that you're the only one I would risk everything for to rescue."

Instantly concerned, Terra's hand lifted to touch his chin. "Oh, Javad. Did he punish you?"

He had, of course. When Vynom discovered that he'd lost the rare healer, he'd nailed Javad to the wall with silver spikes. He'd hung there for weeks, the pain so grinding that he'd begged for death.

Javad grabbed her hand and pressed her fingers to his lips, savoring the sweet taste of her skin.

"It doesn't matter now."

"Javad—"

"We need to get out of here," he interrupted.

Her jaw tightened. Terra was kind and gentle and generous. She was also as stubborn as a mule.

Thankfully, she accepted the need to postpone their reminiscences for later. "Do you have a plan?" she asked.

"Does hope and a prayer count as a plan?"

She stepped close enough to wrap him in the soft warmth of her body. "Yeah, they count."

"Terra."

An aching need blasted through Javad. He'd spent so long battling the instinct to seek out this female and… And what? This. Leaning down, he claimed her lips in a quick kiss of pure hunger. Yes. Desire churned through him. This was what he desired. This, this, this. He deepened the kiss, the heady taste of her plush lips slamming into him with stunning force, like a bolt of lightning. Javad groaned, and his fangs throbbed. Along with another part of his body.

Instinct took over, shutting down his brain as he wrapped his arms around her. It didn't matter that they were in a dank cell. Or that Vynom would soon return. Or even that she had never been meant for him. The warmth of her in his embrace eased an ancient pain he'd carried from the moment he smuggled her out of the fighting pits.

"Javad." She leaned against him, her fingers brushing over his chest before she slowly pushed him away. "We keep getting distracted."

Javad groaned again. This time, it wasn't in a good way. It was more an achy-breaky-gut-wrenching kind of way. Still, while his brain might be misfiring, it wasn't dead.

Terra was right. They had to escape. The sooner, the better.

With effort, he forced himself to move toward the far side of the cell. "I can get us out," he told her, careful not to touch the silver coating the door. "But there are at least four guards at the opening to this cavern."

She moved to stand next to him. "Are they vampires?"

"No." Javad had sensed the demons from the moment he awakened in the cell. "Two trolls. A goblin. And some sort of fey creature."

"I'll deal with them."

Javad blinked. "You?"

"I'm not helpless."

He didn't point out that *he* would hesitate to take on four guards. It didn't matter that they were probably mongrels. Trolls and goblins were fierce warriors, who didn't know the meaning of a fair fight.

Instead, he reminded her that she was a Seraf. "Didn't you take a vow not to harm others?"

She offered him a sweet smile. "Trust me."

Something fluttered in the depths of his heart. "Always."

Chapter 5

Vynom was on his way to the sleeping pens that housed his fighters when he felt a warm breeze creeping over his skin. He snarled, whirling on his heel to glare at the center of the large cavern. There was nothing to see yet, but he knew what was coming.

Dammit. He should never have given the bitch access to get through his magical barriers.

Then again, what choice did he have?

He'd been scraping the bottom of his treasure chest when the heavily cloaked female approached him. She'd been looking for Javad, but he'd refused to tell her where to find his treacherous child. Not without revealing why she was searching for him.

Her answers had been vague, but Vynom had managed to figure out that she hoped to use Javad to get rid of Terra. He didn't ask why she wanted Terra dead. Frankly, he didn't care. All that mattered was that she gave him the perfect opportunity to reclaim his former glory.

His luck had gone in the shitter after Javad had walked away. With the mystery female's help, he would be back on top.

Unfortunately, that included dealing with the tedious bitch on a regular basis.

Clenching his hands into tight balls, he glared blindly toward the source of the scent. The female inside never stepped out of the protection of her portal or revealed herself. As if he hadn't already worked out that she was one of the Serafs from the temple.

So much for their pretense of being peace-loving innocents.

"Now isn't a good time," he growled.

"Tough. Terra is here?"

"Yes." This female had arrived seconds after Javad had been sucked into his cell. She'd warned Vynom to be prepared and disappeared. "Just like you said."

"Good. Have you…?" The female's words trailed away. "Dealt with her?"

"Are you asking if she's dead?"

There was a long silence. Had he managed to anger his unwanted partner with his blunt words? Vynom shrugged. He had what he needed from her. As far as he was concerned, their bargain was at an end.

"Is she?" the female demanded.

"No."

There was a loud hiss. "You promised to take care of my problem."

"I will. But first, I need her."

"For what?"

"She's going to make sure my unruly child fulfills his duty to me," he told her. "Once the fight is over, I intend to make sure both of them are disposed of."

"Then have your stupid fight and be done with it," she snapped.

Vynom scowled. Once upon a time, he could have arranged a fight within a few hours. He had the reputation of matching the toughest, most violent fighters against one another. His establishments were packed to the rafters with eager customers willing to hand over inordinate sums of treasure. Now…

He growled in frustration. "It's not that simple. I have to build maximum anticipation for the battle. The more eager my customers are for the fight, the more they'll be willing to bet."

She clicked her tongue. "I have no interest in your filthy lust for money."

"Well, I have a lot of interest in it," he informed the arrogant pain in his ass. "And I intend to squeeze every bit of gold out of this opportunity."

"Don't be a fool," the female chided. "Terra might be a Seraf, but she isn't without power. You'll regret underestimating her."

Did she just call him a fool? Vynom hid his burst of anger behind a mocking smile. He wouldn't let this female know how easily he could be provoked.

"Chill out. She's safely locked away, along with Javad," he drawled. "By the end of tomorrow night, she'll be dead."

"Don't fail me."

There was another warm breeze, and the portal disappeared. Vynom clenched his hands into fists and continued his journey to the pens.

"Good riddance."

* * * *

Terra carefully peered through the opening at the end of the narrow tunnel. Javad had easily used his powers to crumble the stone around the door, loosening it enough to allow them to squeeze out of the cell. Now, it was her turn to show what she could do.

Her gaze took in the two trolls who were playing some game that involved dice and a lot of grunting. Next to them, the imp tossed a dagger in the air. Near the door, the goblin slouched in a chair. They all wore ragged clothing that appeared to be held together by grime, food stains, and desperate hope. But their shabbiness didn't make them any less dangerous. Just the opposite. Despondency clung to them like a shroud.

"What are you going to do?" Javad asked, his voice a mere whisper.

"Put them to sleep." Terra tapped into her magic.

"All of them?"

"Yes."

"At the same time?"

She ignored his blatant shock. Over the past years she'd grown considerably in her powers, and more importantly, developed the necessary patience to hone and perfect her skills. Now, she reached out to touch the mind of the goblin. It was a tangled mess of hunger, violence, and churning hatred toward his fellow guards. Exactly what she expected from a goblin. Murmuring a soft command, Terra savored the gentle magic that bubbled within her. It felt like champagne fizzing through her veins.

The goblin's eyes slid shut, and Terra turned her attention on the trolls. She released another tingle of magic, and the two slumped forward, hitting the ground with enough impact to send up puffs of dust. With a curse, the imp leaped to his feet, his expression wary as he jerked his head from side to side. Knowing he was about to bolt, Terra hurriedly entered his mind and compelled him to sleep.

He froze, his eyes going blank. Then, with a soft sigh, his knees gave way, and he fell flat on his face.

"That's…" Javad shook his head, the words dying on his lips as he studied the unconscious guards. Then he sent her a glance of pure admiration. "Awesome."

A giddy sense of pride raced through her. As if she'd performed some miracle instead of a routine spell that Serafs used on their patients. She shook her head in disgust. Why did she always act like an idiot when she was near this male?

Because you want to impress him…

The words whispered through the back of her mind, and Terra swallowed a sigh.

Over the long centuries, she'd made a habit of telling herself that her endless dreams of Javad were because he was one of the few males she'd known. She had, after all, spent the majority of her life isolated from the world. Who else would fill her fantasies? But the second she opened her eyes to discover Javad leaning over her, that pretense had been shattered.

The intense joy that had exploded through her had nothing to do with a lack of male companionship, and everything to do with one specific vampire.

Javad was special to her. And if she weren't a Seraf…

"They won't be out for long," she forced herself to say, trying her best to ignore the dark wave of regret that settled in the center of her heart.

Right now, nothing mattered but getting out of the caverns before Vynom realized that they were out of the cell.

"This way," Javad murmured, leading her past the sleeping guards and into the narrow tunnel that led upward.

She had to jog to keep up with his long strides. Not that she would complain. The faster, the better.

"Where are we going?"

"If we can't get out with magic, then we'll do it the old-fashioned way. There has to be an exit somewhere."

She remained silent as they found a narrow flight of stairs carved into the rock and then traveled through several dusty tunnels. Eventually, her curiosity overwhelmed her sense of caution. Once they were free, she would have to return to the temple, and it was very likely that she would never ever see this male again. And...there was more of that dark regret that made her heart feel painfully heavy.

"You said something about coming here to shut down the fighting pits. Did you come alone?"

He slowed as they entered a large cavern so they could walk side by side. "No, I brought along a creature who can see through illusions, but he disappeared when I was sucked through the magical barrier. I assume he's back in Vegas, raiding my personal stash of aged tequila." He grimaced. "I should have sent an army when I heard rumors that Vynom was in my territory. He would have been rooted out and destroyed by now. Instead, I carelessly rushed here to confront him face-to-face. I never considered that this might be a trap." His voice was filled with self-disgust. "Stupid, of course."

She couldn't stop herself from placing her hand on his arm. It was in her DNA to comfort others. And, more importantly, she *ached* to touch him.

"I never thought it would be a trap either," she said, dangerous sensations tingling through her as his muscles rippled smoothly beneath her palm.

Thankfully distracted, he shook off his grim mood. "How did you leave the temple?" he asked.

Terra turned her head as if suddenly fascinated by the strange rock formations dotted around the cavern.

"I told you. I used a portal." She hoped that he would leave it at that.

He didn't.

"I thought Serafs were forbidden from leaving?"

"Yes."

"Yes, you're forbidden from leaving?" he prodded. She nodded. With a muttered curse, Javad came to a halt, reaching to grab her by the shoulders. "Terra. What have you done?"

Reluctantly, she met his gaze that shimmered with hints of bronze. "I made a pledge when I gave you my medallion. I had to keep my promise."

He studied her in confusion. "What about your duty to the temple?"

"It will be there when I return."

"Are you *allowed* to return?"

She released a resigned sigh. Javad was strong and loyal and astonishingly tenderhearted. He was also as stubborn as a rabid hellhound.

"As long as they don't realize I'm gone," she admitted.

His brows arched in surprise. "You snuck out?"

"I did what I had to do."

"Why?"

"It was…" She tried to say, "my *duty*." Or, "*burden*." But the words stuck in her throat.

"For me?" he asked in soft tones.

It was. She'd leaped at the opportunity to be reunited with Javad, risking everything just to see him again.

Rattled by the realization, she pulled out of his light grasp to walk across the cavern. Undeterred by her silent warning that she was done with the conversation, Javad quickly walked up next to her.

"You asked me if my new life made me happy. What about you?" he asked. "Are you happy?"

Happy? It wasn't a word she thought about. She had a destiny. It didn't matter if it made her happy or not.

"I can answer the same as you," she said with a shrug. "When I first returned to the temple, I felt relief. And peace."

"Because you accepted your place in the temple?"

She shook her head. "Because I realized the Matron was right. The world was a big, scary place that destroyed the innocent."

He grimaced, but he was too smart to try and convince her that it wasn't so bad out in the world. After all, they were currently being held prisoner by a vampire who intended to force Javad to fight. Perhaps to the death.

"Why do I sense a *but*?" he asked.

"But eventually, my original frustration returned." She hadn't intended to confess her inner turmoil. This male had no connection to the temple. But there was something in his dark, steady gaze that made the words spill from her lips. As if she were purging them. And maybe she was. "I might have accepted that the Serafs were safer behind the magic of the temple, but that shouldn't stop us from helping the demons who need us."

"I thought demons could petition for healing?"

"Yes. And the Matron decides if they're worthy or not."

He looked confused. "Worthy?"

Terra's lips twisted. That'd been her reaction when she discovered that the demons she healed had been chosen by the Matron. And hundreds, perhaps thousands of others were turned away.

"I've asked her to define the term."

"And?"

"And I spent a month locked in my bedchamber."

Dust filtered from the low ceiling as Javad's burst of temper shook the cavern. "You were imprisoned?"

"Not really," she hastily reassured him. Javad could topple buildings when he was in a mood. Now didn't seem the best time to get him riled up. "I was in a comfortable room with plenty of food and a beautiful view of the gardens." She smiled. "Certainly, it wasn't enough punishment to stop me from nagging about our isolation from the world."

He made a visible effort to control his emotions. "The Matron clearly wasn't prepared for a Seraf like you."

His dry tone made her chuckle. "That's true. I've heard rumors that the Matron sends out scouts to ensure I'm not around when she leaves her private rooms."

His lips parted, but before he could speak, a portal opened over their heads, and something dropped out of the darkness.

Javad shoved her out of the path. "Terra, run!"

She stumbled, grabbing a stalagmite to keep her balance. Whirling around, she watched as the silver net landed directly on top of Javad. He screamed in pain, going to his knees as the metal strands seared deep into his flesh.

"Javad."

Leaping toward the net, Terra was abruptly halted as a humungous troll dropped through the portal, landing directly in front of her. A second later, an icy blast of power filled the cavern as Vynom appeared along with a small fairy, who was no doubt in control of the magical opening.

"Don't let her escape," the vampire snapped, pointing toward Terra. With a grunt, the troll grabbed Terra's arm in a grip hard enough to leave bruises. Vynom narrowed his eyes as he studied her. "And I warn you, Seraf, don't try any funny tricks like the one that has my guards snoring outside the cells. Unless you want Javad fried into a crispy pile of ash."

"No." Her heart lodged in her throat. She didn't need to hear his moans or smell the charred skin to know that he was in gut-wrenching pain. It vibrated in the air. "Please, let him go."

The large vampire ignored her plea, strolling to tower over her. "Ah, sweet Terra. It's been a long time."

She tilted back her head to glare at him. "Not long enough."

"Don't be that way," he chided. "I thought we were old friends?"

"Friends?" She spat the word. "Is that a joke?"

"You were my guest, weren't you? I fed you, clothed you, provided a roof over your head."

"You held me captive."

Vynom clicked his tongue. "Such a nasty word. Besides, it wasn't personal. I needed your skills."

Terra shuddered. She didn't know exactly how long she'd spent in the pits. It'd seemed like centuries, but in reality, it'd probably been less than a year. But during that short time, she'd been forced to heal thousands of fighters, along with whoever happened to be at Vynom's establishment with enough money to pay for her services.

With effort, however, she resisted the urge to remind him of all the horrible things he'd done to her. The male was a ruthless, cold-hearted monster. He didn't know the meaning of regret.

"How did you use my medallion?" she abruptly demanded.

A strange expression tightened his blunt features. "What does it matter?" He motioned toward the troll. "Take her to the main cavern."

"Wait!" Before the oversized demon could haul her away, Terra glanced toward the silver net. "What are you going to do with Javad?"

Vynom curled back his lips to reveal his fully extended fangs. "I'm going to give him the opportunity to become the legend he was supposed to be." He turned his head to stab her with a glare of pure hatred. "Before you."

Terra didn't flinch. Which was impressive, considering the male could crush her with one hand.

"Before me?"

"Javad spent centuries earning his reputation as the most feared fighter in a dozen different dimensions," he snarled. "Demons traveled thousands of miles just to see him in the cage. And then, you arrived."

Terra snorted. Was he serious? He made it sound as if she'd

dropped by for tea. "I didn't arrive. I was kidnapped and sold to you by slavers."

"I shouldn't have bought you," the male complained, like a petulant child instead of a grown demon. "After you arrived, Javad was restless and moody. It only got worse after you disappeared. He clearly mourned your absence. You took away his will to fight."

Oh. Terra blinked, struck by a sudden realization. Vynom's fury wasn't just about losing money. He'd been hurt by what he saw as Javad's betrayal. A brief flare of hope ignited in her heart. Was it possible that she could convince this male to release them?

"He never had the will to fight," she told the male.

"Lies. We were a team. An unstoppable force."

"He did it because you manipulated him into believing it was his duty to fight."

"No. He did it because he was my child. My heir." Ice coated the floor and rimmed the bottom of Terra's gown. "Until you ruined it all."

She softened her tone, attempting to reach any lingering bond the male might feel for Javad.

"He's still your child. Let him go."

There was a second of hesitation, and Terra held her breath. This was the moment. Had she managed to reach Vynom's non-beating heart? The scent of rust thickened in the air, an indication that he was battling a strong emotion. Then, his expression twisted with ugly determination.

"He's my retirement fund." Vynom waved a hand toward the guard. "Take her away."

Chapter 6

Levet had lost track of their journey through the caverns. They'd been forced to retrace their path over a dozen times to avoid the guards who patrolled through the narrow tunnels and dark caves. It made him feel as if they were wandering in circles.

Becoming increasingly wary that he was about to waltz into a trap, Levet halted as Sparkles led him through a narrow crack in the thick stone.

"Wait," he commanded.

Sparkles glanced impatiently over her shoulder. "What's wrong?"

"I smell…" He sniffed again, his wings quivering with sudden horror. "Slave pens."

The fairy smiled. "We have to go through them to reach the maze."

Levet narrowed his gaze. He didn't trust that smile. "Now I smell bullshirts."

"Bullshirts?"

"Tell me where you are leading me."

The female paused as if concocting a plausible lie. Levet folded his arms over his chest, and she sighed.

"I'm leading you to the slave pens."

"I knew it. This is a trap."

Sparkle turned to face him, her face pale and tense. "No, I promise."

"Then why are we down here?"

"My people are locked in cells in the slave pens."

Levet's anger faltered, his heart sinking. He'd spent enough time in various pens to sympathize with any creature stuck inside one.

"How many?"

"Ten."

Levet frowned, sure he'd misheard. "*Ten* frost fairies?"

"We started with thirty."

"Thirty." Oh…goddess. Levet's tender heart squeezed with profound grief. He didn't know the fairies, but he was certain that they were rare and precious and irreplaceable.

"Sometimes, the hellhounds win," Sparkle said in dull tones.

"Mon Dieu."

The fairy reached out her hand in a pleading motion. "Please, please, please. I need your help."

"What do you want from me?"

Sparkle pressed her hands together, her eyes filling with tears. "I managed to escape by hiding in the maze. The crowd assumed I had been eaten and eventually returned to the fights in the main cavern. I've been back down here time and time again, but I don't have the strength to open the door to the cell."

Levet's wings drooped. He was a sucker for tears. "Even if I can release your people from their cells, what good will it do?" He tried to be sensible. There was no point in all of them wandering in circles. "We are still stuck in these caverns. Eventually, we will be discovered."

Sparkle shook her head. "I was telling you the truth when I said there is a tunnel at the end of the maze."

"Why should I believe you?" Levet asked, pretending his heart hadn't already melted into a gloopy mess at the plight of the trapped frost fairies. "You have already proven yourself to be a liar liar pants on fire."

"I didn't lie," the tiny female protested. "I just left out the bit about making a side journey to collect my people before we escape."

Levet sniffed. "A rose that is named a cauliflower is still a rose."

Sparkle blinked. Then blinked again. "What?"

"You lied."

Without warning, the fairy dropped to her knees. "I beg you. Name any price, and I will pay it if you help my people," she pleaded in husky tones. "If I don't get them out, they will die."

Levet heaved a sigh. He'd been a goner from the second the female appeared.

"You are fortunate that I am a knight in shining armor," he

muttered.

"You'll release them?"

Levet shrugged. "It is what heroes do."

With a cry of relief, Sparkle sprang to her feet and rushed to throw her arms around Levet.

"Thank you!" She planted soft kisses over his face.

Levet turned his head. He enjoyed kisses as much as the next male. Probably even more. But he no longer wanted them from every female who happened to find him irresistible—which, he had to admit, was most of them. He was, after all, a most magnificent gargoyle. But for the past few months, he had a singular preference for Inga's lips. Or he *would* have if the stupid ogress would ever bother to kiss him.

"No need for that." He gently untangled himself from the fairy's clinging arms. "Lead the way to the slave pens."

* * * *

Javad hissed as the silver net was roughly tugged off his body.

Grueling pain pulsed through him, sapping his strength as he struggled to heal from the deep burns. He had only a vague recollection of being hauled through the darkness. And then what seemed like an eternity of lying on a stone floor with the net covering him. The only thing he was certain of was that Terra was nowhere around.

"Terra." Clenching his fangs, he forced himself to a seated position, glancing around the small cave. He ignored Vynom, who stood over him, and allowed his senses to flow outward. Immediately, he detected the guards just outside the opening, and above them, the choking smell of dozens of demons. Perhaps hundreds of them. That had to be where the cage match would be held. The huge crowd made it impossible for Javad to pinpoint Terra's soft aloe vera scent. "Where is she?"

"Right now, Javad, you need to worry about yourself," Vynom warned.

"Where is she?" he stubbornly repeated.

Vynom's blunt features twisted as if angered by Javad's concern for the female.

"Safe. For now." Vynom crouched down, studying Javad with an expression of contempt. "Such a disappointment."

"I could say the same."

The older male ignored Javad's insult. "The one thing I admired about you was your ruthless ability to concentrate on your goals. Nothing ever distracted you. Not greed. Not friends. Not even females. It made you the perfect fighter."

"I'm not interested in history," Javad snapped. He never thought about his time in the pits. It had been a dull, painful existence that wasn't worth remembering.

"I just have one question," Vynom pressed.

"What?"

"Why her?"

"Her?"

"The Seraf," Vynom clarified. "Why was she your Achilles heel?"

Javad shook his head, realizing that the male truly believed that Terra had been a curse to Javad. No doubt because his rotten, corrupt heart couldn't imagine the beauty of caring for another being.

"You're wrong," Javad said.

"About what?"

"You believe Terra was a weakness."

"She was," Vynom insisted. "She destroyed you."

"She gave me the courage that eventually set me free." Javad held the male's gaze. "Without her, I would still be a prisoner because of my twisted sense of loyalty."

Vynom surged upright, his icy fury frosting the air. "I made you."

Javad remained on the floor. He sensed he was going to need every ounce of strength he could muster.

"You used me."

"You think that Viper would have taken you in if it weren't for the fact that I was your sire?" Vynom snarled.

Javad arched a brow. "What are you talking about?"

"He's been trying to punish me for centuries. You were just another tool to bring about my destruction."

"Why would he want to punish you?"

Vynom shrugged, his eyes smoldering with a toxic brew of emotions. "Jealousy, obviously."

Javad swallowed a laugh. The male was unhinged if he thought Viper was jealous. The clan chief of Chicago ran an empire of demon clubs around the world, while Vynom had barely been able to manage a small-time fighting pit.

Then a sudden suspicion niggled at the back of his mind. There was no way Viper was jealous of Vynom, but the clan chief might have decided the male needed to be punished. Not only for how he'd treated Javad, but the other fighters as well. It was no secret that Viper detested bullies. That might very well be the reason for Vynom's downfall.

A strange warmth flowed through Javad at the thought.

"Viper respects me," he said, his pride unmistakable. "Just as I respect him."

Vynom muttered a foul curse. "Let's hope he respects his next manager just as much," he sneered. From above them, the strike of a gong resounded, echoing and expanding as the sound traveled through the tunnels. "It's time."

"Time for what?" Javad asked.

"Your grand finale."

Icy dread shot down Javad's spine. "I thought I was going to be given time to prepare."

Vynom's lips twisted. "I may be down on my luck, but I'm not stupid. Even though I wanted to get as much buzz as possible for the fight, I'm not going to risk having you escape. I'm cashing in while I can."

Javad grimaced as Vynom spun on his heel and marched out of the cave. Cashing in? Grand finale?

Neither sounded good for him.

Chapter 7

Javad had been right.

There was nothing good about being forced into a pair of black leather pants and thigh-high boots with his hair pulled into a tight braid. He looked like a stripper in a cheap Vegas club. And there was definitely nothing good about being led up the stairs to enter the enormous chamber now filled with cheering demons.

In the center of the space stood a large cage, constructed of iron bars and a canvas mat. It was attached to a foundation of stones so it could tower over the crowd. Javad was led past the bleachers and up a ramp by two goblins who were directly behind him with silver daggers pressed against his back.

With his head held high, Javad entered the cage and heard the door clang shut behind him. It was a familiar sound. Just like the shouts from the gathered demons were familiar. And...

And that scent.

Terra.

Javad tilted back his head, gazing to the top of the cage where Terra was standing next to a huge troll, who was tightly gripping her arm.

Javad's fury at seeing her being manhandled by the oversized brute was tempered by the relief that she was alive and seemingly unharmed. The sheer intensity of his response revealed the depth of his fear that she'd been hurt.

Their gazes locked, and he watched her desperately shake her head as if she were pleading with him not to fight. He sent her a smile that he hoped was reassuring before turning his attention to the orc across the wide canvas mat.

Frack was a monster. Not a fairy tale creature with blue fur and googly eyes. He was a seven-foot mountain of pure muscle, thick hide, claws, six-inch tusks protruding from his lower jaw, and crimson eyes. He was naked, although various spots were covered by armor that had been magically embedded in his skin.

It left way too much hanging in the breeze for Javad's taste.

"Hello, Frack. Long time no see," he drawled. "Although I'd like to see a lot less. Did you forget your pants? I'll wait if you want to go and find them."

As expected, Frack bellowed in fury and recklessly charged. The orc's sense of humor was as lacking as any amount of intelligence. It was depressingly easy to provoke him.

Javad stood still as Frack barreled toward him. There wasn't much finesse about the way the orc fought. He was all muscle and primitive instinct. Above him, Javad heard Terra cry out in fear, but he waited. It wasn't until he could smell the orc's foul breath that he finally leaped straight into the air, kicking Frack in the face. The sound of crunching bones echoed before Javad flipped over the demon's head and landed lightly on his feet.

"Bad leech." Frack growled, whirling to reveal the blood dripping from his snout.

Javad wasn't stupid enough to think he'd actually wounded the demon, but he had Frack foaming at the mouth. The more he infuriated the creature, the more likely it was that he would take stupid risks.

"I see you have a few more armor bits attached," Javad said, pretending to admire the metal while he judged the best way to get through it. The only way to kill the orc was to cut off his head. An impossible task without a magically enhanced weapon. Or to cut through the heart that was located in his lower stomach. "Getting soft in your old age?"

Frack snarled and charged again. Javad waited for the orc to get close before he kicked out. This time, however, he didn't bother aiming for the head. The demon's skull was as thick as a brick wall. Instead, he smashed his heel into the armor covering the demon's lower stomach.

The satisfying sensation of the armor denting beneath the blow traveled up his arm. Unfortunately, the price of getting so close to the beast was being unable to avoid the arm the size of a tree trunk that slammed into his side.

The blow cracked Javad's ribs and sent him flying across the cage to smack into the iron bars. Another bone snapped in two.

Javad hissed in pain, ignoring the roar of the crowd as he regained his balance and started to circle the orc, breathing through the agony. He needed a few seconds to heal his wounds.

"When was the last time you bathed?" Javad taunted. "You smell like a rompo demon after feasting on a rotting hellhound."

Frack scowled as he awkwardly turned to keep his wary gaze on Javad. "Stay still, leech."

Javad flashed his fangs in a direct challenge. "You want me? Come and get me."

On cue, Frack bent low and lumbered forward. He intended to use his skull as a battering ram, but Javad easily skipped to the side, once again kicking at the armor. This time, the metal split, the sharp edges digging into the orc's thick hide. Frack howled in pain, but with surprising speed, he slashed out with his claws, scoring deep gashes into Javad's side.

Javad grimaced. He'd managed to injure Frack, but he was incurring too much damage in return. His hours wrapped in the silver net had drained his strength, making it harder than it should be for him to heal.

If he were going to try and make an escape, he had to do it now.

Pretending to charge toward the waiting orc, he used his momentum to leap up and grab the top of the cage. Then, with sheer brute strength, he pulled apart the iron bars to make a wide enough space to crawl through.

"Javad." Terra struggled to move toward him, only to be jerked back by the troll holding her captive.

Fury raced through Javad, distracting him just long enough for Frack to grab his leg.

Shit. Javad tried to pull himself through the opening, but Frack had all the leverage. Not to mention a couple hundred extra pounds of muscle.

With a savage yank, Frack had Javad away from the bars and was carrying him over his head like a trophy. The crowd went nuts, screaming for Javad's death.

So much for my adoring fans, Javad wryly acknowledged.

Struggling to break free of the orc's crushing grip, Javad was helpless as the bastard bent his arms to ram his tusks into Javad's back.

The razor-sharp weapons sliced through Javad's flesh, leaving a gaping wound.

Javad could feel his blood draining away at an alarming rate. Dammit. He had to do something. Now.

Closing his eyes, Javad concentrated on his powers, releasing just enough to cause a small fissure beneath the cage. The sharp sound of cracking stones echoed. Frack grunted as if confused by the tremor beneath his feet. Thankfully, the creature didn't have the brains to realize the danger he was in. It wasn't until more cracking sounded followed by a loud snap as the thick foundation abruptly split that he finally sensed the peril. By then, it was too late. The cage tilted, and he was forced to release Javad as he tumbled backward.

Landing heavily on the mat, Javad struggled to his feet. The crowd screeched for Frack to end the battle, but all Javad could hear was Terra's soft cries of horror from above.

Frack took a second longer to shove himself upright, snarling in frustration as he stomped forward.

"Me squash you."

Javad could sense the last of his energy draining away, but a flare of hope raced through him as he caught sight of the blood that leaked from beneath Frack's armor. The creature's assumption that he was impervious to harm just might be the means for Javad to win the battle.

Javad motioned toward the orc, his smile taunting. "You can try."

Frack lumbered forward, smiling in anticipation as Javad pretended to be too weak to avoid the attack. Then, wrapping his arms around Javad, he squeezed him in a brutal grip. Javad ignored the excruciating pain of his bones snapping as he focused on his last hope of defeating the creature.

Curling his fingers, he rammed his fist into the armor. Over and over, he pounded at the same spot, forcing the metal deeper into the orc's body.

The crowd noise receded, and his sight began to narrow as he started to black out. Still, he continued hitting the metal, driving it through the flesh and into the soft heart. Abruptly, the stench of orc blood filled the air.

Frack shrieked, belatedly realizing the danger. He released Javad and gazed down in horror at the destroyed bit of his shield. The creature had been so certain that he was protected, he could only gape in confusion as his life drained from his body.

Javad struggled to stay upright, knowing that he'd won the battle as Frack dropped to his knees and then fell flat on his face with a mighty thump.

This was it. He'd defeated his enemy. It was time to escape. All he had to do was leap toward the opening at the top of the cage and grab Terra.

Then they could...

They could...

Javad swayed, his brain filled with fuzz as he glanced up to see Terra stretching out her hand toward him.

He'd always known they could never have a happy ending. She was a Seraf who was trapped in her crystal temple, while he was a vampire stained with the blood of his opponents. Just like Romeo and Juliet, they were destined by fate to be forever parted.

The sappy thought faded away as blackness consumed him, and he tumbled on top of the orc.

* * * *

The crowd went wild as Javad collapsed. As if the sight of the two bloody and broken demons was the greatest thing in the world. Terra cried out, trying to jerk from the troll's grip. She was desperate to get to Javad.

At the same time, Vynom entered the cage, smiling with cocky delight at the carnage he'd created.

The...scumbag.

Waving his arms, he encouraged the screams of raw violence. At last, the shouts died away, and Vynom moved to kick the dead orc in the head.

"As I promised, the battle of the century!" There was a brief roar of approval. "But I also promised you a once in a lifetime surprise," Vynom continued, holding up a wooden stake. "An opportunity for the highest bidder to claim the honor of killing Javad the Vanquisher."

Terra's blood ran cold as the demons jumped to their feet.

"Ten gold coins," shouted a voice from the back.

"Twenty," another answered.

"Fifty."

"One hundred."

Terra blocked out the bids being shouted by the crowd, a slow calm coming over her. When she'd still been in the fighting pits in Athens, Javad had entered a room where she was healing an imp who'd had his ribs shattered by a blow from an ogre. He watched in silence as she'd peeled back the flesh to inspect the damage before healing the ribs and knitting the skin back together. When she was finished, he'd asked her why she didn't use her magic to fight against the demons holding her captive. She'd told him that she had sworn a pledge when she was taken to the Seraf temple. No matter what happened, she would never use her powers to harm another.

Even if it meant saving her own life.

But this time, it wasn't her life in danger.

It was Javad's.

And no pledge or promise or destiny would stop her from doing everything in her power to save him.

Closing her eyes, Terra sank into the magic that bubbled inside her. It was light and bright and glorious. It was also potent. Concentrating on the troll's fingers digging into her arm, she used the connection to send her magic into the demon. It swirled and fizzed, dancing through his bloodstream until it reached his heart.

Terra opened her eyes and turned her head to watch as the troll frowned. He could feel the magic, but he would have no way of knowing where it was coming from or what it was doing.

Not until his heart came to an abrupt halt.

The creature's eyes bulged, his mouth dropping open, and his skin changing to a weird blue color as he struggled to breathe. Terra turned away, pulling her arm from his loosened grasp.

The troll wouldn't die. Or at least, she didn't think he would. She'd never used her magic like that before. But he would be incapacitated for the next few minutes, at least. Long enough for her to escape.

Leaping forward, she dove headfirst through the space Javad had created between the bars. She managed to twist as she dropped through the air, landing on her feet next to Javad.

A stunned silence filled the vast chamber, every gaze locked on her as she lifted her hand. Clearly, they expected her to perform some magnificent feat of magic. Even Vynom stepped back in shock.

Ah, if only it were so easy.

Her magic wasn't magnificent. It was barely more than functional.

But the breathless sense of anticipation gave her the opportunity that she needed. Waving her hand in a grand, flamboyant motion, Terra created a portal. She couldn't get through the magical barrier, but she could take them to another part of the caverns.

Pulling Javad through the opening, she slammed it closed and glanced around.

They were away from the crowd, but that didn't mean they were safe. With care, she lowered the unconscious vampire onto the hard ground and quickly inspected the cramped cave to make sure there were no hidden dangers. There was no sense rescuing Javad from one deathtrap only to land him in another.

She'd just managed to convince herself that they were safe for the moment when a familiar smell caught her attention. What the heck? She glanced around, her brow furrowed. Then, bending down, she scooped an object off the ground and held it in the palm of her hand.

What was going on?

Momentarily lost in her dark thoughts, Terra was distracted by the sound of a soft moan. Shoving away the questions that thundered through her, Terra tucked the object into the pocket of her gown and rushed back to Javad.

"Javad." She dropped to her knees beside him.

He hissed in pain as he forced his eyes open. "Terra?"

"I'm here."

He studied her in silence as if trying to memorize each line and curve of her face. Then, he grimaced. Was it another wave of pain? Terra's heart squeezed with fear.

"Where are we?" he demanded.

"Somewhere in the caverns," she said. "I think it's close to where we were being held in the cell."

"How did we get here?"

She brushed her fingers over his face. His skin was icy to the touch and far too pale. Even for a vampire.

He was fading fast.

"I can open a portal to places inside the magic barrier," she told him, trying to keep the fear out of her voice. Panicking wouldn't help. Right now, it was up to her to protect Javad. "I just can't get us out of here."

"Good." Relief flared through his eyes. "There has to be an exit nearby. Go."

She wiped the blood droplets from his cheek. "No."

"Eventually, they're going to find us." His voice was harsh, his face twisting with frustration. "You have to leave."

"Not this time," she stubbornly insisted. "I walked away once. I won't do it again."

"Terra." With obvious effort, he reached up to cup her face in his hand. "You don't belong here. You have to return to the temple."

Terra's jaw clenched before she managed to control her burst of anger. "I will. In time," she promised, calmly pulling up her sleeve. "First, you need to drink."

Javad's hand dropped, his face blank. As if she'd just hit him with a shovel instead of offering him the elixir that would lure him back from the brink of death.

At last, he gave a stiff shake of his head. "No. I can't."

Stubborn vampire. She leaned forward, holding out her arm.

"I may not be capable of healing you with my magic, but my blood will help you regain your strength," she insisted.

He turned his head, looking tragically noble with his battered body and expression of agonizing need.

"You don't know what it means."

Her lips twitched. She hadn't seen this melodramatic side of Javad before. It was cute.

"That I'm your mate?"

He froze as if shocked by her blunt question. "Okay, maybe you do know."

"I've always known." And she had. From the very first time she'd seen him. But it was a knowledge she'd hidden deep in her heart. A vampire had one mate, and once he or she had taken the blood of their destined partner they were bound together for eternity. "I just couldn't allow myself to acknowledge our bond. Not when we were destined to be separated."

Regret shimmered in his eyes. "It's no different now."

"Everything is different."

He couldn't miss the fierce edge in her voice. "What do you mean?"

She lowered her lashes, trying to hide the dark, tangled emotions that boiled and churned like a thundercloud just waiting to burst open.

"I broke my vow," she revealed, her voice low and carefully calm. "I hurt the guard holding me so I could escape."

"Terra."

She lifted her gaze to study his horrified expression. "It's okay. Really."

"No." He grabbed her hand, squeezing her fingers. "Being a Seraf is who you are."

His words whispered through the air, and Terra braced herself for the pain. From the day she was born, she'd known that she was destined to join the Serafs in the fabled temple. She was celebrated in her tribe, and her parents had been given a fine home and piles of treasure.

Even arriving at the temple had been filled with pomp and ceremony. She'd been treated as if she were the most special creature on the face of the Earth.

Having that stripped away should have been devastating.

Instead, all she felt was…peace.

"I'll always be a Seraf, whether I'm at the temple or not," she told him in a firm voice. "My healing abilities aren't dependent on the Matron. Or living among other Serafs." She pressed her hand to the center of her chest, directly over her heart. "It's here."

Javad shook his head in regret. "This is my fault."

"No," she sternly chided. "This is Vynom's fault."

"If I—"

"Ssh." Terra was done arguing. Pressing her inner wrist against his mouth, she leaned down to whisper in his ear. "Drink, or I won't have anyone to protect me when they manage to track us down."

He paused, seemingly caught off guard by her less than subtle manipulation. "You don't fight fair," he complained.

She smiled. "I'm learning. Better late than never."

"I suppose that's true." His fingers drifted down her arm in a light caress. "But I don't want you to become a cynic."

The distant thunder of running footsteps could be heard. It sounded like a hundred demons stampeding overhead.

The search was on.

"I won't become anything if you don't heal," she reminded him. "We're running out of time."

Holding her gaze, Javad allowed his fangs to lengthen. They gleamed with a snowy whiteness despite the shadows, emphasizing the razor-sharp tips. Terra shivered, but not with fear.

There was nothing but breathless anticipation as those lethal fangs pressed against her skin. Then, with one sharp jolt of pain, they pierced through her flesh and sank deep.

She gasped, burying her face in his hair that tumbled free of the braid. His cool, enticing male scent surrounded her as the sting faded and an exquisite feeling of pleasure flooded her. She could feel each deep draw as he drank her blood, the sensation shockingly erotic. Almost as sensual as the hand that slid up her arm to wrap around her shoulder, urging her to lay down beside him.

Keeping her wrist pressed against his mouth, Terra scooted down, arching against the hard length of his body.

"Javad." His name came out on a shaky sigh, her head cradled in the curve of his throat. Then, barely aware of what she was doing, she bit and licked away the blood that trickled down his neck.

The taste exploded as it slid down her throat, intensifying her acute awareness of the male beside her.

Already, she could sense his savage wounds healing. She wasn't using her Seraf powers. She didn't need to. She could feel his pain easing and his strength returning. As if they were connected... No. It was more than a mere connection. It was as if they'd become one body. One soul. One heart.

Forever intertwined.

Awareness shuddered through her, and she arched closer to his bare chest. She wanted to halt time. To savor the mating magic as it rushed through her with intoxicating intensity. Javad's arm tightened around her, perhaps sharing the same dreamy wish. Then, with a low groan, he withdrew his fangs and stared at her in wonderment.

"Terra," he murmured. A mysterious smile curved his lips as he held up his arm to reveal the crimson tattoo that ran beneath the skin of his inner forearm. "*My* Terra."

Terra smiled as she studied the intricate pattern that looked too delicate to be real. Then she held up her own arm, not at all surprised to discover a matching design. She'd felt the tingling sensation as the tattoo formed. A visible symbol of her mating with Javad.

"Yes, yours," she agreed.

His eyes shimmered a pure bronze as he hesitantly reached out to trace her mark with the tips of his fingers.

"How?"

She chuckled, turning her head to brush her lips over the bare skin of his chest. "Did you think I could be your mate without you being mine?"

"It happens."

"Not between us." She snuggled closer. "We were bound together from the moment our paths crossed."

Chapter 8

Levet had never considered himself a snarly sort of demon. Unlike the leeches or dragons or even the Weres, he wasn't forever moaning and groaning about the tiniest problem. Indeed, he was infamous for his perky charm.

But after an hour of roaming the musty caves with a dozen frost fairies, he wasn't feeling very spirited. In fact, his nerves had reached the breaking point.

Why had he opened the door to their prison cell? Granted, their gratitude had been effusive. They'd cheered and danced and even made up a spontaneous song to herald his greatness. Levet had memorized the words. When he returned to Vegas, he was going to hire a bard to stroll behind him while singing it. How else could people know about his latest daring adventure?

Unfortunately, things had gone steadily downhill.

The fairies stopped singing as they left the slave pens, but they were soon bored. The excitement of escaping was forgotten as they trudged through the dark tunnels. Within a few minutes, they were squabbling and complaining and even throwing rocks at each other. It was like trying to herd a gaggle of drunk frat boys. Hmm. Did humans travel in gaggles?

Levet heaved a loud sigh as two of the fairies tumbled past him, fighting over a worthless crystal that one of them had found on the floor.

"Could they possibly make more noise?" he muttered.

Sparkle fluttered her wings, looking confused. "You want them to be louder?"

"*Non.* I was being..." He sighed again. Fairies would be fairies. Flighty. Impulsive. Noisy. "Never mind. How much farther to the maze?"

"Not far, but don't forget, it is guarded by hellhounds. We'll have to find a way to distract them," Sparkle warned.

Levet halted. He wasn't afraid of mangy hellhounds. He was a hero, after all. But having to sneak past them didn't fill him with tingly joy. Especially if they hadn't been recently fed. There was nothing pleasant about being trapped in the belly of a hellhound.

There had to be another way.

Glancing around, he noticed a large crack in the wall of the tunnel. It was too narrow for the massive head of a hellhound to fit through. Even better, he could feel a faint breeze, and that meant it opened into a cave. Or perhaps another tunnel.

He pointed toward the crack. "We can go that way."

Sparkle leaned forward, sniffing the breeze. She stiffened, her eyes wide. "No. I smell a vampire."

Levet had already caught the familiar scent. "*Oui.* Javad."

Sparkle tilted her head. "What's a javad?"

"A friend." Levet stepped forward and wiggled into the crack. "I hope," he muttered.

* * * *

Javad knew that he should have some regret.

A mating was one of the most significant events that could happen in a vampire's life. It was meant to be a glorious celebration enjoyed in as much luxury and decadence as possible. Instead, they were lying on a stone floor, covered in dust, and being hunted by his looney-ass sire.

Regret, however, was the last thing he felt.

Burying his face in Terra's hair, he shivered as stunned joy blasted through him. He'd spent so many centuries convinced that he would never be reunited with this female. *His* female. She had her duty as a Seraf, hidden behind the walls of the temple. It would take time for him to accept that she really was his.

He brushed his lips down her cheek, briefly savoring the sweet taste of aloe vera before he forced himself to pull back and study her delicate features.

"As much as I want to pretend that we're alone in the world, we need to get out of here."

She nodded, rising to her feet. Javad frowned as he watched her sway. How much blood had he taken? Enough to heal himself, although he remained dangerously weak.

"Are you okay?" he asked as he flowed upright and grasped her arm.

"I'm fine."

"Not for long," a male voice drawled as Vynom appeared through the opening on the far side of the cave. "You cost me a lot of money, Seraf."

Javad wrapped a protective arm around Terra. He was still too weak from his battle with Frack to directly attack his sire, but Vynom couldn't know that. The older male would have to be cautious until his backup band of mercenaries arrived.

"You had your battle," he snapped, trying to catch the scent of any nearby demons.

Nothing yet, but it was only a matter of time.

"I want more," Vynom stepped forward, a sneer twisting his lips even as he kept a wary gaze locked on Javad.

"More what?" Javad demanded.

"He was auctioning off the chance to put a stake through your heart while you were unconscious," Terra muttered.

Javad curled his lips in disgust. "Classy as always, Vynom."

The male shrugged. "I'm a survivor."

"Just another way of saying you're an immoral, spineless coward who will sacrifice anything and anyone to make a buck," Javad taunted.

Vynom narrowed his eyes, the air chilling to a temperature expected in the Arctic, not Nevada.

"Did you call me a coward?"

"I'm pointing out the obvious." Javad covertly glanced toward Terra. She seemed...distracted. Her head was turned toward the far wall, her brow furrowed as if she were concentrating on something that he couldn't see.

Was she attempting to create a portal? Damn, he hoped so.

Vynom took another cautious step forward. "The only obvious thing is that you chose the wrong path. We could have ruled the world together."

Javad rolled his eyes. He'd been with Vynom for centuries, and never once had the male treated him as more than an object to bring in the crowds. Certainly, he hadn't considered him a partner.

"Yeah, thanks, but no thanks. I'm happy with my club in Vegas."

A layer of ice suddenly coated the ground. "Perhaps you're right," Vynom spat. "I tried to believe that you were worthy to stand at my side, but you're a small, pathetic demon who deserves to die in this barren cave."

The older male held up his hand to reveal the wooden stake he had clutched in his fist.

Javad muttered a frustrated curse. His strength was returning, but not nearly fast enough.

"Terra, now might be a good time to think about getting out of here."

She seemed oblivious to the approaching danger as she studied the wall. "Fairies."

He arched his brows. "What?"

"And...a gargoyle."

Javad's confusion abruptly cleared. He didn't know anything about fairies, but only one gargoyle could possibly be in the caverns.

"Levet."

The scent of granite drifted through the air, along with shrill voices that sounded as if they were arguing. And was that...singing?

There was a brief second of chaos as the tribe of fairies swarmed out of the crevasse. Javad took swift advantage, unleashing a small burst of power that shook the cavern beneath Vynom's feet. The male snarled as he leaped back, obviously assuming that the floor was about to crack open. Instead, the ceiling over his head shattered and showered him in jagged boulders.

Vynom crumpled to the ground, covered in stony rubble. He wasn't dead, but he was knocked out. At least, for the moment.

"Oh, there you are." Levet waddled forward, absently polishing the tip of his tail.

"Where have you been?" Javad demanded.

"Exploring."

Javad scowled down at the miniature pest. "I was being held hostage, and you were on a tour?"

Levet blew a kiss. "Did you miss me?"

Javad shuddered. "Like a stake through the heart."

Levet pursed his lips, leaning forward to sniff Javad's arm. Javad scowled. What was wrong with the strange creature?

"Stop that," he snapped.

"You're mated!" the gargoyle exclaimed, glancing toward Terra, who watched him with a bemused expression. "I am Levet." He offered a deep bow. "KISA. At your service."

Terra blinked. "KISA?"

"Don't ask," Javad growled.

"Knight in shining armor," Levet announced in proud tones.

"He truly is a knight in shining armor." A tiny, pale-haired fairy appeared next to the gargoyle. "He rescued my people."

"It is what I do." Levet smiled smugly at Javad before introducing his companion. "This is Sparkle. She's a frost fairy. Have you heard of them? They're super rare." Levet winced as shrill shouts came from the fairies across the cave. They had gathered in a circle to watch two males who were apparently wrestling over some small stone. "And loud. Really, really loud," Levet muttered.

Javad clenched his fangs. Was he being punked? It was hard to believe there could be any creatures more annoying than the gargoyle.

"Can you get us out of here?" he demanded, raising his voice to be heard over the shouts.

Sparkle nodded, pointing toward a door on the other side of the cave. "There is a tunnel that will lead us to the surface," she said.

Levet nodded. "We just need help digging it out."

A flare of hope eased the knot in Javad's stomach. Was it possible that they might get out of the caverns?

"Fine, lead us to it," he commanded.

"Javad!" On cue, Vynom regained consciousness. Digging himself out of the rocks, he rose to his feet.

Javad braced himself for the attack. He wasn't at full strength, but he was growing stronger every second.

Concentrating on his sire, Javad was only vaguely aware of the cries of alarm from behind him. He didn't have time to worry about the fairies. It wasn't until they ran screaming past him, holding long, pointed icicles that he realized they weren't fleeing in horror. Nope, they were headed straight for Vynom.

"Monster," Sparkle cried in her high voice, jabbing the icicle into

Vynom's lower stomach.

Vynom cursed, tossing aside the fairy, but ten others swarmed him like ants on honey. And each possessed a needle-sharp weapon they stabbed into him over and over. In the blink of an eye, he was leaking blood from a hundred wounds.

Roaring in fury, Vynom wind-milled his arms, trying to knock away the tiny attackers. But the creatures were surprisingly tenacious, returning to the battle even when it appeared they were grievously injured.

Standing next to the stunned Javad, Levet cleared his throat. "Is he a friend of yours?"

"He's..." A smile curved Javad's lips as Vynom dropped to the ground, dying by a million pinpricks. "He's nobody."

It was a fitting end.

* * * *

It took them less than an hour to dig through the tunnel thanks to Javad's brute strength and Levet's explosive fireballs. Then, leaving the gargoyle surrounded by the chattering frost fairies, who eagerly insisted that he return to their homeland as some sort of hero, he stepped into the portal that Terra formed.

Now, after a quick tour of the Viper's Nest to give Terra a sense of where they would be staying, along with feeding his mate the finest ambrosia and nectar to be found in Vegas, they retired to his private apartments that were deep underground so they could each shower away the grime from Vynom's caverns.

Javad paced through the long living room that was surprisingly cozy with wood-paneled walls, an open-beamed ceiling, and thick rugs on the floor. After endless centuries of Vynom's gaudy taste, he craved simplicity. Even the furniture had been chosen for comfort and not style. The low, sturdy sofa and chairs had thick ivory cushions and matching pillows. The only decoration was the exquisite tapestry that hung on the far wall. The delicately stitched scene was that of an oasis in the desert with a midnight sky speckled with stars. It'd been a gift from Viper when he first opened the club and was one of Javad's most prized possessions.

He was on number thirty—or was it forty—of his circuits around the room when Terra at last entered. She wore a gold silk bathrobe that matched his own—compliments of the Viper's Nest. It hit her mid-thigh and clung to her slender curves to perfection, creating an explosion of heat in his lower stomach.

Halting in the center of the carpet, Javad watched as Terra walked toward the tapestry, studying it with seeming interest before continuing toward the plain wooden bookcase.

At last, Javad could take it no longer.

Having her so near sparked a fire of need inside him. The sweet scent of aloe vera swirled through the air, along with a lemony shampoo that clung to her damp hair. He *ached* to have her in his arms. In his bed.

But more importantly, he desired to know that she was pleased with his lair. She'd sacrificed so much to offer him the healing potency of her blood. Her home. Her family. And the duty that had been the essence of her life since she was very young.

The fear that she might be unhappy in this place was gnawing at him like cancer.

"Well?" he at last demanded.

Terra turned around, her brows lifted in confusion at his sharp tone. "Well what?"

His lips twisted as he moved to stand directly in front of her. He couldn't remember his life as a human, but he presumed the fluttering nerves in the pit of his stomach were what it'd been like to have a crush on a young maiden.

Or maybe a young male. Who knew what had pleased him during those years?

"You know that I'm desperate to hear you say that you love this place," he said, framing her face in his hands. "And that you intend to spend the rest of eternity here with me."

"This is your home."

"Yes."

She smiled, wrapping her arms around his waist and snuggling her face against his chest.

"And now it's my home."

He bent his head, resting his cheek on the top of her head. He trembled, as much from her soft words as from the delicious heat of her body that soaked through his skin and eased the tension that cramped his muscles.

"You can be happy here?" He kissed her damp hair, his fingers trailing down the curve of her spine. "It's not too dark? Or sparse? Or—?"

She chuckled, pulling back to press her fingers against his lips. "As Goldilocks said…it's just right."

He stared down at her upturned face. "You're just right," he murmured.

And she was. It wasn't just the delicately carved features, or the narrow nose and lush lips. Or even the stunning lavender hue of her eyes. It was the kind gentleness that radiated from her and surrounded her like a halo.

It had called to him like a siren's song from the second he caught sight of her. Back then, he'd convinced himself that his soul was too jaded for her innocence. He'd wanted her protected. Even from himself.

Now… Now, he was going to hold her so tightly, she would never escape.

Her fingers traced his lips, the soft caress sending sparks of pleasure shooting through him.

"I'm not going to argue with that," she assured him.

"Good." He grasped her hips, maneuvering her until her back was flat against the wall. "We have better things to do with our time," he assured her.

Her lips twitched, her fingers drifting down to wiggle inside the vee of his robe. Her touch was light, but it scorched him with pure bliss.

"Do we?" she teased, fingers continuing their trek downward as if she were fascinated by the feel of his skin.

"Oh, yes," he rasped.

"You mean this?"

Holding his gaze, Terra grasped the lapels of his robe and jerked it open. Then, with a firm motion, she peeled it off his body. Dropping it to the floor, she looked smug.

A startling burst of joy raced through Javad at the same time his lust hurtled into hyperdrive. Well, well, well. Who could have known his sweet Seraf was such a tease? The glimpse of her naughty humor was like receiving a rare, unexpected gift.

One he intended to treasure.

"That's a start." He tilted his head down to capture her lips in a soft, seeking kiss as he removed her robe and tossed it across the room.

She trembled, but it wasn't with fear. He could smell the rich scent of desire that perfumed her skin.

"There's more?" she whispered.

"Much more." With a fluid motion, Javad swept his mate off her feet and cradled her against his chest. "Much, much, much more."

Her lavender eyes shimmered with anticipation as he carried her into the adjoining room. He wasn't the kind of male who had to have a soft bed and silk sheets to enjoy sex. The more adventurous, the better, as far as he was concerned. But their mating had been on a rock floor in a dank cavern. He'd be damned if their first time together was anything but perfect.

He strode across the glossy wood floor to the large bed that had been hand-carved from teak. There was a matching armoire and a heavy trunk where he kept his weapons. Above them, a muted light spilled from a bronze and crystal chandelier.

With gentle care, he lowered her onto the mattress and straightened to simply appreciate the sight of her. Damn. Nothing had ever been so beautiful as the shocking contrast of her golden hair spilling across the black duvet and the pale limbs that appeared to have been carved from the finest marble.

She was a work of art...

And his. All his.

A growl rumbled in his throat as he moved to lay beside her. Then, pulling her into his arms, he pressed her against his body.

"Terra." Hunger clawed through him at the feel of her satin-soft skin and delicate curves.

"Oh," she breathed as if in shock.

Javad instantly froze, lifting his head to gaze down at her. "Is something wrong?"

She hesitantly brushed her hands over his chest. "I can feel what you do."

Ah. From the moment of their mating, they'd started to share a bond. It began with being able to sense what the other was feeling. But the longer they were mated, the more intense the connection would become, allowing them to physically share the sensation of each other's touch.

He combed his fingers through the golden silk of her hair. "Does that bother you?"

A soft sigh fell from her parted lips. "It's astonishing."

"Astonishing," he muttered, absorbing the echo of her pleasure as it reverberated inside him. "Yes. That's exactly what it is." He kissed a path down her jaw. "And glorious." He paused at the base of her throat, directly over her racing pulse. "And exciting." Using the tip of his fang, he pricked the delicate skin, lapping the droplet of blood. Another blast of hunger wrenched a groan from his lips. "And delicious."

"Delicious?"

"Mmm." He pressed the hard length of his cock against her lower stomach. "Like the finest champagne."

She wrapped her arms around his neck, tangling her fingers in his hair. "I spent so many centuries fantasizing about being in your arms. This doesn't seem real."

"I had the same fantasies." He pulled back a bit to study her bewitching beauty. "I dreamed of how the torchlight would shimmer in your golden hair." His fingers teased the sensitive tips of her nipples until she gasped in pleasure. "And the soft perfection of your skin." He lowered himself to brush a light kiss to her lips. "And your sweet scent that drives me crazy."

She arched toward him in invitation. "How crazy?"

He chuckled, then used the tip of his fang to trace the curve of her neck. Terra groaned, her hands lifting to thread her fingers in his hair.

"Hang on tight," he warned.

"That sounds dangerous," she breathed.

"Nothing but pleasure, I promise."

"I trust you."

Her words were as intoxicating as her enticing heat that wrapped around him like a caress.

This female was so tiny and vulnerable beneath him. He could crush her with one blow. Or drain her dry before she could stop him. But as he lifted his head to study her, there was nothing in her eyes beyond a smoldering lavender desire.

Holding her gaze, he brushed his fingers over the ugly brand on her shoulder. Vynom's mark.

"Nothing will ever hurt you again."

She nodded. "As long as we're together, I'll never be afraid."

Unable to resist temptation, Javad sank his aching fangs into the pillowy softness of her breast. Terra hissed at the combination of pleasure and pain. Javad ran his hands down her body in a soothing motion as he sipped her blood.

Her taste hit his tongue with a heady warmth. *She's more addictive than any drug*, he silently acknowledged.

Feeling her tremble as her passion threatened to overwhelm her, Javad reluctantly pulled his fangs out and gently licked closed the tiny wounds.

Eventually, he would drink from her while their bodies were entwined. But for their first time together, he wanted to concentrate on ensuring that she was drowning in heart-stopping, bone-melting, unforgettable joy.

"Javad," she murmured with breathless anticipation, gliding her fingers down his back.

He turned his attention to her puckered nipples. The scent of aloe vera drenched the air, but he wanted more. Using his tongue and the sharp tips of his fangs, he teased the sensitive nubs until she squirmed in bliss.

"Faster," she complained.

He chuckled in delight, skimming his lips down her shivering body.

"All good things, in good time," he promised.

She tugged at his hair. "The early bird gets the worm."

His startled laugh echoed through the room. "What?"

"I don't know," she muttered, her face flushed with passion. "I'm not thinking very clearly right now. I just want…"

"What?"

"You," she breathed. "I want you."

Her words punctured his unbeating heart, melting it into a puddle of goo.

"You got me, Terra," he swore in soft tones.

She gave another yank on his hair. "All of you."

"Yes. But first…"

With a slow, wicked smile, he parted her legs and wiggled down the mattress until he was kneeling between them. Instantly, he was surrounded by the sweet scent of her arousal. His mouth watered, though his hunger was no longer for blood.

Gripping her hips, he licked through her slick heat, feeling a smug satisfaction as he wrenched a loud groan from her throat. His nymph liked that. A lot.

Using her soft moans as a guide, he dipped his tongue inside her, driving her desire higher and higher, taking her to the edge before easing away and starting all over again.

"Enough."

With unexpected strength, Terra reached down to grab his shoulders and hauled him upward.

Javad readily gave in to her impatience.

As much as he enjoyed hearing the sound of her soft pants, his need was spiraling toward the point of no return. He wanted to be deep inside her when that happened.

"I like when you're bossy," he teased, kissing the upper curve of her breast before gliding up the slope of her throat.

Her skin was damp with sweat, and the lemony scent of her hair teased his nose.

Delicious.

"Good." She framed his face in her hands as she wrapped her legs around his waist. "Get in me. Now," she ordered.

Javad didn't have to be told twice.

Holding her smoldering gaze, he pressed the tip of his rock-hard cock into her body. They groaned in unison, the pleasure so shocking that it made the world come to a screeching halt.

Time ticked away as Javad simply savored the sensations that battered his body. Anticipation. Ecstasy. And a love so profound that his heart didn't feel big enough to contain it.

Releasing a shaky sigh, Terra scored her fingernails down his chest, then with a smoldering smile, she lifted her head to lick away the small trail of blood.

Hunger slammed into Javad. With a harsh growl, he plunged his erection deep into her body.

"Yes," she urged in a husky voice, lowering her hands to cup his ass as he drove into her with enough force to rock the bed.

She met him thrust for thrust, proving that she wasn't nearly as fragile as she appeared.

Thank the goddess. Javad wrapped her tightly in his arms, savoring her sharp cry as her body shuddered in blissful release.

Javad thrust again, his back arching as his orgasm ripped through him with titanic force.

Damn.

Collapsing onto the mattress next to his mate, Javad pulled her tight against his trembling body.

"My Terra," he murmured, pressing a kiss to the top of her tangled curls.

She snuggled against his chest, closing her eyes as she drifted to sleep.

"Forever."

Epilogue

Standing in the living room of their private apartment, Terra brushed her hands down the gown she hadn't worn for two weeks. It felt...weird. And not in a good way. Still, she'd been waiting for this particular moment since she returned to Vegas. She wasn't going to miss it because her nerves were tangled into painful knots.

Easily sensing her tension, Javad moved to capture her hands in his cool grip. He was dressed in a pair of loose black slacks and a gold tunic embroidered with rubies.

"Are you sure you're ready for this?"

She smiled, instantly calmed by his touch. Or maybe she was just distracted. What female wouldn't be sidetracked by an insanely sexy vampire regarding her with such heart-wrenching concern?

She squared her shoulders. "It's time."

Javad frowned. "You're being very mysterious."

"I just need to tie up a few loose ends," she said.

She'd been deliberately vague when she told Javad that she had to return to the temple. As much as she adored this male, he was more than a little protective. If he thought that she was walking into danger, he would be in hyper-vampire-mode. She didn't want to terrify the Serafs until she could discover the truth.

"You're sure?" he demanded.

Terra studied Javad's face. His concern about traveling to the temple was easy to read, but something else was troubling him. Something she could sense through their mating bond.

"What do you mean?"

"It would be understandable if you have..." His gaze lowered to their entwined fingers as if searching for the appropriate word.

"Regrets."

"Regrets about what?"

"Leaving the temple."

Understanding hit Terra with stunning force. Javad wasn't just concerned. He was worried that she missed her life as a Seraf.

Stepping forward, she framed his face in her hands and stared into his dark, beautiful eyes.

"Never," she assured him in a voice that rang through the room with unshakable confidence. "Nothing has made me as happy as being your mate, Javad. You're stuck with me for the rest of eternity."

A stiffness drained from his body as he leaned down to press his mouth tenderly against her lips.

"Thank the goddess," he rasped.

Terra shivered, excitement fluttering through her at the sharp press of his fangs. Less than an hour ago, she'd been in the shower when Javad entered to wrap her in his arms. Before the shower was done, she had her legs wrapped around his waist, and those fangs had been buried deep in her throat.

She swallowed a moan. Just the thought was enough to make her fingers itch to rip off his clothes and tumble him onto the nearby sofa.

"Let's go before you distract me," she murmured, stepping back.

His smile was smug. "I like distracting you."

That was no lie. Over the past two weeks, he'd done just that, several times a day... Her answering smile was more than a little smug as well as she lifted her hand and opened a portal.

As soon as she stepped through, however, her easy expression disappeared.

The familiar smell of wildflowers wrapped around her along with the dazzling morning light that poured through the glass walls of the temple. The sun didn't concern her. This was a place of magic. Javad wouldn't be hurt by the sunshine. She did, however, quickly glance around to make sure there weren't any unexpected visitors that might be dangerous.

Nothing.

Well, nothing beyond the crowd of white-robed Serafs gathered around the tall, gaunt-faced female with dark golden hair that was braided and folded like a crown on the top of her head.

The Matron.

Terra had chosen this particular moment because she knew that it was the traditional day of welcoming for the newest Serafs. It was the one time everyone gathered at the center of the temple.

There was a stir of curiosity as Javad stepped out of the portal, his arm instantly wrapping around her shoulders in a protective motion.

The older female stepped forward, her face hard as she took in Terra with a disapproving gaze. "You."

Terra offered a stiff nod of her head. "Matron."

The sound of a gasp could be heard as Cyra stepped from behind the Matron to study Terra in disbelief.

"Terra." She pressed her hands to her chest. "I feared that you would never return."

Terra forced her lips into a humorless smile. "Sorry I'm late. I was detained by a savage vampire who intended to kill me."

Cyra's gaze flicked toward Javad. "That vampire?"

"No." Terra pressed closer to her mate. "Javad saved me."

The Matron stiffened her spine, pressing her hands together. "No matter what he's done to earn your gratitude, you have no right to desecrate our temple by bringing him here," she snapped, her eyes blazing with fury. "Yet another example of your lack of respect for the Serafs."

Terra met the Matron's glare with one of her own. "What exactly should I respect?" She waved a hand. "A fancy temple? Pretty gardens? Your bulging treasure chests?"

"That is enough."

"Brace yourself. I'm just getting started."

The Matron frowned. "I have no idea what you're talking about."

"Did you tell the new recruits that you dole out our gifts to the highest bidder?"

"I take care to choose who can enter our temple," the Matron informed her in stiff tones. "It is my duty to protect my people."

Terra snorted. "You barter us for profit."

A buzz of whispers erupted from the Serafs behind the female. Like the rustle of leaves in a soft breeze.

The Matron's jaw tightened. "That's not true. You just admitted that you left the tower and were attacked. Is that what you want for your sisters?"

"Of course, not," Terra instantly denied. "The temple is important to keep them safe. But there's no reason we can't offer our help to everyone who petitions for it. Or even travel through the world with proper guards to ensure that we aren't hurt."

The Matron flushed. "Blasphemy."

It was a word that Terra had heard with monotonous regularity over the past centuries.

"No." She pointed toward the vast emptiness that surrounded them. "This is blasphemy. This place should be filled with Serafs treating those in need. We should have lines of petitioners out the door. Instead, we huddle here alone, waiting for someone with enough wealth to purchase our blessing. We aren't angels of mercy, we're mercenaries."

More buzzing from the sisters arose as the Matron's face turned a dark shade of puce.

"I won't be lectured by you." She pointed a finger toward the portal that Terra had left open. Better safe than sorry. "Get out."

"I will." Terra sucked in a deep, calming breath. Enough. Arguing with the Matron was a frustrating, worthless waste of time. And not the reason Terra had come here. "As soon as I finish what I came here to do."

The Matron frowned. "What are you talking about?"

"I was kidnapped and held hostage by a vampire named Vynom—"

"Because you left my protection," the older female interrupted.

Terra shook her head. "I was lured there when someone used my medallion."

"That's ridiculous. No one could use it," the Matron protested.

"No one but another Seraf," Terra corrected.

"Another Seraf?"

"That's what I said."

The female stiffened, a wary expression on her narrow features. "Who?"

"We're about to find out." Terra reached into her pocket to pull out the strand of hair that she'd found in the cavern after escaping the cage with Javad. She held it up so everyone could see. "Whoever was working with Vynom left behind a clue."

Closing her eyes, Terra muttered a simple spell. There was a tingle of magic in the air, and she opened her eyes to watch the hair float off her palm before gliding toward the Matron. Then, bypassing the leader of the Serafs, it twirled and landed on Cyra's head. Terra's heart squeezed even as she gave a sad shake of her head. The traitor had been obvious the moment Terra had caught the scent of aloe vera and found the hair.

After all, it was Cyra who'd brought the medallion to her. And promised to hide Terra's disappearance from the temple. Still, it hurt even more than Terra expected. She'd thought Cyra was her friend. Instead, the female had done everything in her power to destroy Terra.

"I hoped my suspicions were wrong," she whispered. "How could you?"

Cyra's eyes darted from side to side as if she were desperately trying to think up a convincing lie. Then, clearly realizing that she'd been caught red-handed, she tilted her chin to a defiant angle.

"You were tearing us apart," she accused Terra.

"Cyra." The Matron swiveled her head to stare at the younger female in horrified disbelief. "Did you conspire with a vampire to harm one of your sisters?"

Cyra held out a pleading hand. "I had to get rid of her, Matron."

"Why?"

"The younger Serafs were becoming restless." She nodded toward the crowd currently watching them with avid gazes. "More and more of them were questioning your decisions, and some even whispered of finding a new Matron to lead them. A revolt was brewing. The only way to save what you built was to get rid of the source of their discontent."

"Traitor!" The cry came from somewhere at the back of the room, and the Matron winced.

Glancing toward her flock, the Matron quickly judged the mood that was rapidly tilting from confused to angry. With surprising speed, she reached out to grasp Cyra's arm and nodded toward Terra.

"Come with me."

The Matron marched across the floor, dragging Cyra behind her. Terra started to follow, but with a blur of movement, Javad was suddenly blocking the Matron's path.

"Be very careful, Matron," he warned, his eyes smoldering with a bronzed glow. "I will destroy you if you so much as look at Terra wrong. Got it?"

The Matron flinched. Smart Seraf. Javad's fangs were fully extended and ready to do serious damage.

"I'm not going to hurt her. I swear," the Matron said, waving an unsteady hand toward the nearby opening. "We'll go in there."

In a tight group, they entered the small library that smelled of old leather and sandalwood. Terra took a deep breath, savoring the scent. She'd often taken refuge in this place when her frustration threatened to goad her into doing something stupid. There were few things more relaxing than hours spent lost in a good book.

Once inside, Javad shut the door and moved to stand next to the Matron. It was an unspoken threat.

The older female, however, was concentrating on Cyra, who was wiping away her tears.

"Child. What have you done?"

Cyra folded her arms around her waist. "I did it for you," she told the Matron. "For the temple. You said we had to stop Terra. So I did."

There was a long stretch of silence as the Matron's color drained from her face. She looked almost sick.

"For me," she breathed.

Without warning, Cyra had dropped to her knees, holding her hands out in a silent plea for understanding.

"We can't let her lead the others astray, Matron." Cyra's eyes glittered in a frenzied way. As if she were on the verge of hysteria. Or madness. "Once she's dead, we can convince the others—"

"Sleep." The Matron spoke the word, and Cyra tumbled to the floor, her eyes closed, and her body slack.

There was another bit of tense silence as they stared down at the unconscious female. Then Terra turned her attention to her former leader.

"Cyra plotted to kill me, but the blame lies on your shoulders, Matron," she said in harsh tones.

Expecting more excuses, or even accusations to turn the blame away from her, Terra was caught off guard when the Matron slowly nodded.

"Yes."

Terra blinked in surprise. "Excuse me?"

"You're right." Spinning away, the female paced toward the towering bookcases that lined the walls. The hem of her silken robe brushing the handwoven carpet was the only sound that broke the silence. She seemed lost in thought, her head bowed as if carrying a heavy load. Then slowly, she turned and lifted her head to study Cyra. "I allowed my fear of your power among the younger Serafs to infect Cyra with a toxic desire to protect me."

Terra's brows snapped together. Had the Matron been dipping into the nectar? That was the only way she could make that particular accusation.

"I'm just one of the sisters. I have no power."

The female's lips pinched in frustration. "You've been a disruptive force that has had the temple in chaos since the day you arrived."

"That's ridiculous."

"She's not wrong," Javad murmured, his lips twitching. "You've been a disruptive force in my life since the night we met."

The Matron ignored Javad, her exasperated gaze locked on Terra. "Your calls for change continued to ripple through the other Serafs, even after you disappeared. You and your progressive ideals gained in popularity no matter how hard I tried to quash the uprising."

Terra smiled. "Good."

"Is it? You weren't there to watch as we were slaughtered by those we tried to heal. To have your sisters die in your arms. Or to huddle in hidden bunkers while we were being hunted like animals by those who wanted our blood."

Terra's smile faded. At times, she allowed her fervent desire to return the Serafs to what they *should* be to rule and forgot that there'd been genuine reasons for building the temple.

"No." Her voice was soft with regret. "It must have been terrifying."

The Matron pressed her hands together. "I made a solemn pledge two thousand years ago to do everything I could to keep my children safe."

"A worthy goal, but it's turned us into prisoners." Terra spread her arms. "We have to be free to share our gifts. And to choose our own paths."

The Matron parted her lips as if to argue with Terra's plea, then, glancing back down at Cyra, she heaved a resigned sigh.

"Any change will take time," she muttered.

Terra's heart skipped a beat. She wasn't a fool. It would take decades, maybe centuries for the Matron to give in to the inevitable need to transform the temple. But at least it was a start.

"What will you do with Cyra?" Terra demanded.

She was still deeply hurt by the betrayal of her former friend. It had been as painful as any injury she'd received in Vynom's less-than-tender care. But she couldn't bear the thought of Cyra being judged and condemned as a traitor.

The Matron grimaced. "She'll have to be punished, but I can't destroy her."

With a low growl, Javad moved forward. He wasn't nearly so forgiving. Terra hurriedly stepped in front of him, placing her hands on his chest.

"No, Javad," she pleaded as she tilted back her head to meet his fierce glare. "Cyra is no longer my concern. Just as Vynom is no longer yours." She ran her hands up his chest to circle her arms around his neck. "Nothing matters but our future." She went up on tiptoe to brush her lips across the line of his stubborn jaw. "Together."

He snarled out a curse, but slowly, his tense muscles eased. She planted another kiss on his chin before she turned to face the older female, who regarded her with a wary expression.

"You're leaving?" the Matron asked.

Terra leaned back against Javad, savoring his strength. How had she existed without him?

"Yeah, I have a new life in Vegas now."

The Matron offered a stiff nod. "I won't insult your intelligence by pretending that I'm sad to see you go. But I do promise to consider what I've learned today."

"Change is inevitable. You can lead it or be crushed by it," Terra warned, glancing over her shoulder at the male who'd forever altered her life. "Are you ready?"

He smiled, his arms wrapping around her waist. "Let's go home."

"Home."

Without bothering to glance toward the grim-faced Matron, Terra lifted her arm and opened a portal.

Together, they stepped out of the past and into the future.

* * * *

Also from 1001 Dark Nights and Alexandra Ivy, discover Slayed by Darkness, Blade, Rage/Killian and Kayden/Simon

Sign up for the 1001 Dark Nights Newsletter
and be entered to win a Tiffany Key necklace.

There's a contest every month!

Go to www.1001DarkNights.com to subscribe.

Discover 1001 Dark Nights Collection Seven

Visit www.1001DarkNights.com for more information.

THE BISHOP by Skye Warren
A Tanglewood Novella

TAKEN WITH YOU by Carrie Ann Ryan
A Fractured Connections Novella

DRAGON LOST by Donna Grant
A Dark Kings Novella

SEXY LOVE by Carly Phillips
A Sexy Series Novella

PROVOKE by Rachel Van Dyken
A Seaside Pictures Novella

RAFE by Sawyer Bennett
An Arizona Vengeance Novella

THE NAUGHTY PRINCESS by Claire Contreras
A Sexy Royals Novella

THE GRAVEYARD SHIFT by Darynda Jones
A Charley Davidson Novella

CHARMED by Lexi Blake
A Masters and Mercenaries Novella

SACRIFICE OF DARKNESS by Alexandra Ivy
A Guardians of Eternity Novella

THE QUEEN by Jen Armentrout
A Wicked Novella

BEGIN AGAIN by Jennifer Probst
A Stay Novella

VIXEN by Rebecca Zanetti
A Dark Protectors/Rebels Novella

SLASH by Laurelin Paige
A Slay Series Novella

THE DEAD HEAT OF SUMMER by Heather Graham
A Krewe of Hunters Novella

WILD FIRE by Kristen Ashley
A Chaos Novella

MORE THAN PROTECT YOU by Shayla Black
A More Than Words Novella

LOVE SONG by Kylie Scott
A Stage Dive Novella

CHERISH ME by J. Kenner
A Stark Ever After Novella

SHINE WITH ME by Kristen Proby
A With Me in Seattle Novella

And new from Blue Box Press:

TEASE ME by J. Kenner
A Stark International Novel

FROM BLOOD AND ASH by Jennifer L. Armentrout
A Blood and Ash Novel

QUEEN MOVE by Kennedy Ryan

THE HOUSE OF LONG AGO by Steve Berry and MJ Rose
A Cassiopeia Vitt Adventure

THE BUTTERFLY ROOM by Lucinda Riley

Discover More Alexandra Ivy

Slayed by Darkness
A Guardians of Eternity Novella
By Alexandra Ivy
Coming June 22, 2021

Only an idiot would try to kidnap Jayla. She's a take-no-prisoner kind of vampire who rebelled against the previous King of Vampires, and now regularly battles with both human and demon enemies who resent the success of Dreamscape casino she manages in Hong Kong. So when she's snatched off the streets, she doesn't bother to struggle. Instead she starts plotting her slow, bloody revenge.

The last creature she expects when she arrives at her destination is Azrael, the mysterious mercenary vampire she killed a century ago.

Azreal has never forgotten Jayla, and not just because she tried to stab a stake through his heart. He'd never encountered a female who could match him in battle. Her raw courage was sexy as hell. And it didn't hurt that she was drop-dead gorgeous. But, he didn't abduct her because he desired her. Or at least, that wasn't his main motivation. He needs her rare talent to stop time. An evil fey has stolen his sword. The weapon is magically bound to him, and unless he retrieves it, he's doomed to a painful death.

* * * *

Blade
A Bayou Heat Novella
By Alexandra Ivy & Laura Wright

Sexy Suit, Blade was held captive and abused for decades. Benson Enterprises was desperate to use his superior blood to create super soldiers. But when he's finally rescued, he can't return to the Wildlands with the other prisoners. Not without the female he was forced to watch being impregnated. The female who has gone missing.

Beautiful and broken, Valli just wants to run away and never look back. But with the shocking news of her pregnancy fresh in her mind, she wonders if that's even possible. Told by her captors that one of the caged animals assaulted her, she knows she must do everything in her power to keep her unborn child safe. But when a glorious male tracks her down and claims her and her baby as his own, will she have the strength to walk away?

* * * *

Rage/Killian
Bayou Heat Novellas
By Alexandra Ivy and Laura Wright

RAGE

Rage might be an aggressive Hunter by nature, but the gorgeous male has never had a problem charming the females. All except Lucie Gaudet. Of course, the lovely Geek is a born troublemaker, and it was no surprise to Rage when she was kicked out of the Wildlands.

But now the Pantera need a first-class hacker to stop the potential destruction of their people. And it's up to Rage to convince Lucie to help. Can the two forget the past—and their sizzling attraction—to save the Pantera?

KILLIAN

Gorgeous, brutal, aggressive, and *human*, Killian O'Roarke wants only two things: to get rid of the Pantera DNA he's been infected with, and get back to the field. But the decorated Army Ranger never bargained on meeting the woman—the female—of his dreams on his mission to the Wildlands.

Rosalie lost her mate to a human, and now the Hunter despises them all. In fact, she thinks they're good for only one thing: barbeque. But this one she's guarding is testing her beliefs. He is proud and kind, and also knows the pain of loss. But in a time of war between their species, isn't any chance of love destined for destruction?

* * * *

Kayden/Simon
Bayou Heat Novellas
By Alexandra Ivy & Laura Wright

ENEMY TO LOVER:

Kayden is obsessed with revenge after his parents disappeared when he was just a cub. Now the gorgeous Hunter has discovered the man responsible for betraying them - Joshua Ford - and it's time for payback. Beginning with the kidnapping of Joshua's daughter, Bianca. But last thing he expects is to be confronted with the horrifying realization that Bianca is his mate. Will he put revenge before his chance for eternal happiness?

BEAUTY AND THE BEAST

Sexy male model, Simon refuses to give up his exciting life in New York City to return to the slow heat of the Wildlands. For a decade, many Pantera have tried to capture the rogue Diplomat and bring him home, but all have failed. Now it's Tryst's turn. The hard, brilliant, and gorgeous, Hunter is the ultimate tracker. But can the admitted beast-girl of the Wildlands capture her prey without losing her heart in the process?

Shades of Darkness

Coming November 20, 2020!
Go to https://alexandraivy.com for more information.

"A hundred bucks you can't finish it in one drink," the vampire drawled.

Chaaya flicked a dismissive glance over the potent demon liquor that burned with a blue fire. It wasn't the first time she'd been challenged since she'd strolled into the elegant casino.

It was easy to underestimate her. She looked mortal with her delicate features, her large, dark eyes and soft pink lips. Her skin was bronzed, and her dark hair was buzzed close to her skull to reveal the Celtic tattoos that started behind her ears and ran down the sides of her neck.

She wore a black leather jacket and matching pants that couldn't disguise just how tiny she was compared to the other demons in the place. And while she had a copper spear with a short ebony handle belted to her side, she looked like easy prey.

Which was why she was constantly being tested.

"Two hundred," she demanded.

The vampire grinned, revealing his snowy white fangs. He was a tall, red-haired male with the perfect features that were shared by all vampires. He also had the usual arrogance.

"Done."

Chaaya tapped a slender finger on the table, waiting for the demon to show his money. The vampire hissed, but he reached into the front pocket of his slacks and pulled out a stack of crisp one hundred-dollar bills. He peeled off two and dropped them on the table.

"There."

Chaaya reached for the grog and with one flick of her wrist she tossed the flaming liquid down her throat. She swallowed, bracing herself as the grog hit her stomach with the force of an exploding volcano. Once she was certain she wasn't going to pass out, she wiped her lips with the back of her hand and reached for the money.

"Done."

The smirk on the vampire's overly-pretty face changed to disbelief. "What are you?"

She shrugged. "Just a girl who can't say no," she murmured, rising to her feet. She tossed a couple dollars on the table. "Here, have a drink on me."

She strolled away from the puzzled creature, heading toward the roulette table across the crowded room. She borrowed a few thousand dollars from Basq's private stash he kept hidden in his bedroom. Before the night was over, she intended to double her ill-gotten fortune. Or lose it all.

Either way, it was all good.

Basq would be pissed. Chiron would have heartburn. And she would have enjoyed a night of entertainment that was different from her usual drunken escapades at the tawdrier demon clubs.

Win. Win. Win.

She was passing by a brightly lit stage where a pair of frost fairies were performing a sensual dance that included a lot of fluttering wings and sparkles when a hand reached out to grab her upper arm.

Chaaya halted, slowly swiveling her head to glare at the male who'd dared to touch her without permission.

He wasn't old in vampire terms. Maybe a couple hundred years. Chaaya wasn't sure how she knew, but she could sense a demon's age in the lack of power that surrounded them. This one was slender with blue eyes and skin as pale as snow. His dark hair was slicked back to emphasize the arrogance of his finely chiseled features.

Chaaya deliberately lowered her gaze to the fingers digging into her flesh.

"Are you tired of that hand being attached to your arm?" she asked in sweet tones.

"I just want to talk to you," the male retorted, stupidly maintaining his tight grip. "I haven't seen you around here before."

Chaaya covertly reached for the copper spear. Since her return to this world she'd discovered that she attracted a lot of attention. From both males and females. But she wasn't at the Viper's Nest to make friends. Or even enemies, which was a lot more fun.

She was there to release some pent-up steam. Period.

About Alexandra Ivy

Alexandra Ivy graduated from Truman University with a degree in theatre before deciding she preferred to bring her characters to life on paper rather than stage. She started her career writing traditional regencies before moving into the world of paranormal with her USA Today, Wall Street Journal, and New York Times bestselling series The Guardians of Eternity. Now she writes a wide variety of genres that include paranormal, erotica, and romantic suspense.

Text ALEXANDRA to 24587 to receive text alerts whenever a new release comes out!

Visit https://alexandraivy.com for more information.

Discover 1001 Dark Nights

Visit www.1001DarkNights.com for more information.

COLLECTION ONE

FOREVER WICKED by Shayla Black
CRIMSON TWILIGHT by Heather Graham
CAPTURED IN SURRENDER by Liliana Hart
SILENT BITE: A SCANGUARDS WEDDING by Tina Folsom
DUNGEON GAMES by Lexi Blake
AZAGOTH by Larissa Ione
NEED YOU NOW by Lisa Renee Jones
SHOW ME, BABY by Cherise Sinclair
ROPED IN by Lorelei James
TEMPTED BY MIDNIGHT by Lara Adrian
THE FLAME by Christopher Rice
CARESS OF DARKNESS by Julie Kenner

COLLECTION TWO

WICKED WOLF by Carrie Ann Ryan
WHEN IRISH EYES ARE HAUNTING by Heather Graham
EASY WITH YOU by Kristen Proby
MASTER OF FREEDOM by Cherise Sinclair
CARESS OF PLEASURE by Julie Kenner
ADORED by Lexi Blake
HADES by Larissa Ione
RAVAGED by Elisabeth Naughton
DREAM OF YOU by Jennifer L. Armentrout
STRIPPED DOWN by Lorelei James
RAGE/KILLIAN by Alexandra Ivy/Laura Wright
DRAGON KING by Donna Grant
PURE WICKED by Shayla Black
HARD AS STEEL by Laura Kaye
STROKE OF MIDNIGHT by Lara Adrian
ALL HALLOWS EVE by Heather Graham
KISS THE FLAME by Christopher Rice
DARING HER LOVE by Melissa Foster
TEASED by Rebecca Zanetti
THE PROMISE OF SURRENDER by Liliana Hart

MIDNIGHT UNLEASHED by Lara Adrian
HALLOW BE THE HAUNT by Heather Graham
DIRTY FILTHY FIX by Laurelin Paige
THE BED MATE by Kendall Ryan
NIGHT GAMES by CD Reiss
NO RESERVATIONS by Kristen Proby
DAWN OF SURRENDER by Liliana Hart

COLLECTION FIVE
BLAZE ERUPTING by Rebecca Zanetti
ROUGH RIDE by Kristen Ashley
HAWKYN by Larissa Ione
RIDE DIRTY by Laura Kaye
ROME'S CHANCE by Joanna Wylde
THE MARRIAGE ARRANGEMENT by Jennifer Probst
SURRENDER by Elisabeth Naughton
INKED NIGHTS by Carrie Ann Ryan
ENVY by Rachel Van Dyken
PROTECTED by Lexi Blake
THE PRINCE by Jennifer L. Armentrout
PLEASE ME by J. Kenner
WOUND TIGHT by Lorelei James
STRONG by Kylie Scott
DRAGON NIGHT by Donna Grant
TEMPTING BROOKE by Kristen Proby
HAUNTED BE THE HOLIDAYS by Heather Graham
CONTROL by K. Bromberg
HUNKY HEARTBREAKER by Kendall Ryan
THE DARKEST CAPTIVE by Gena Showalter

COLLECTION SIX
DRAGON CLAIMED by Donna Grant
ASHES TO INK by Carrie Ann Ryan
ENSNARED by Elisabeth Naughton
EVERMORE by Corinne Michaels
VENGEANCE by Rebecca Zanetti
ELI'S TRIUMPH by Joanna Wylde
CIPHER by Larissa Ione

RESCUING MACIE by Susan Stoker
ENCHANTED by Lexi Blake
TAKE THE BRIDE by Carly Phillips
INDULGE ME by J. Kenner
THE KING by Jennifer L. Armentrout
QUIET MAN by Kristen Ashley
ABANDON by Rachel Van Dyken
THE OPEN DOOR by Laurelin Paige
CLOSER by Kylie Scott
SOMETHING JUST LIKE THIS by Jennifer Probst
BLOOD NIGHT by Heather Graham
TWIST OF FATE by Jill Shalvis
MORE THAN PLEASURE YOU by Shayla Black
WONDER WITH ME by Kristen Proby
THE DARKEST ASSASSIN by Gena Showalter

Discover Blue Box Press

TAME ME by J. Kenner
TEMPT ME by J. Kenner
DAMIEN by J. Kenner
TEASE ME by J. Kenner
REAPER by Larissa Ione
THE SURRENDER GATE by Christopher Rice
SERVICING THE TARGET by Cherise Sinclair
THE LAKE OF LEARNING by Steve Berry and MJ Rose
THE MUSEUM OF MYSTERIES by Steve Berry and MJ Rose

On Behalf of 1001 Dark Nights,

Liz Berry, M.J. Rose, and Jillian Stein would like to thank ~

Steve Berry
Doug Scofield
Benjamin Stein
Kim Guidroz
Social Butterfly PR
Asha Hossain
Chris Graham
Chelle Olson
Kasi Alexander
Jessica Johns
Dylan Stockton
Richard Blake
and Simon Lipskar

Made in the USA
Middletown, DE
21 August 2020